HAPPY NARWHALIDAYS

BEN CLANTON

EGMONT

JINGLE SHELLS, JINGLE SHELLS, JINGLE ALL THE WAY!

WHILE SWIMMING IN THE BAY! JINGLE SHELLS, JINGLE SHELLS, JINGLE ALL THE WAY!

OH WHAT FUN IT IS TO SING

'TIS THE SEASON

OH, WHAT FUN
IT IS TO SING
WHILE . . . .

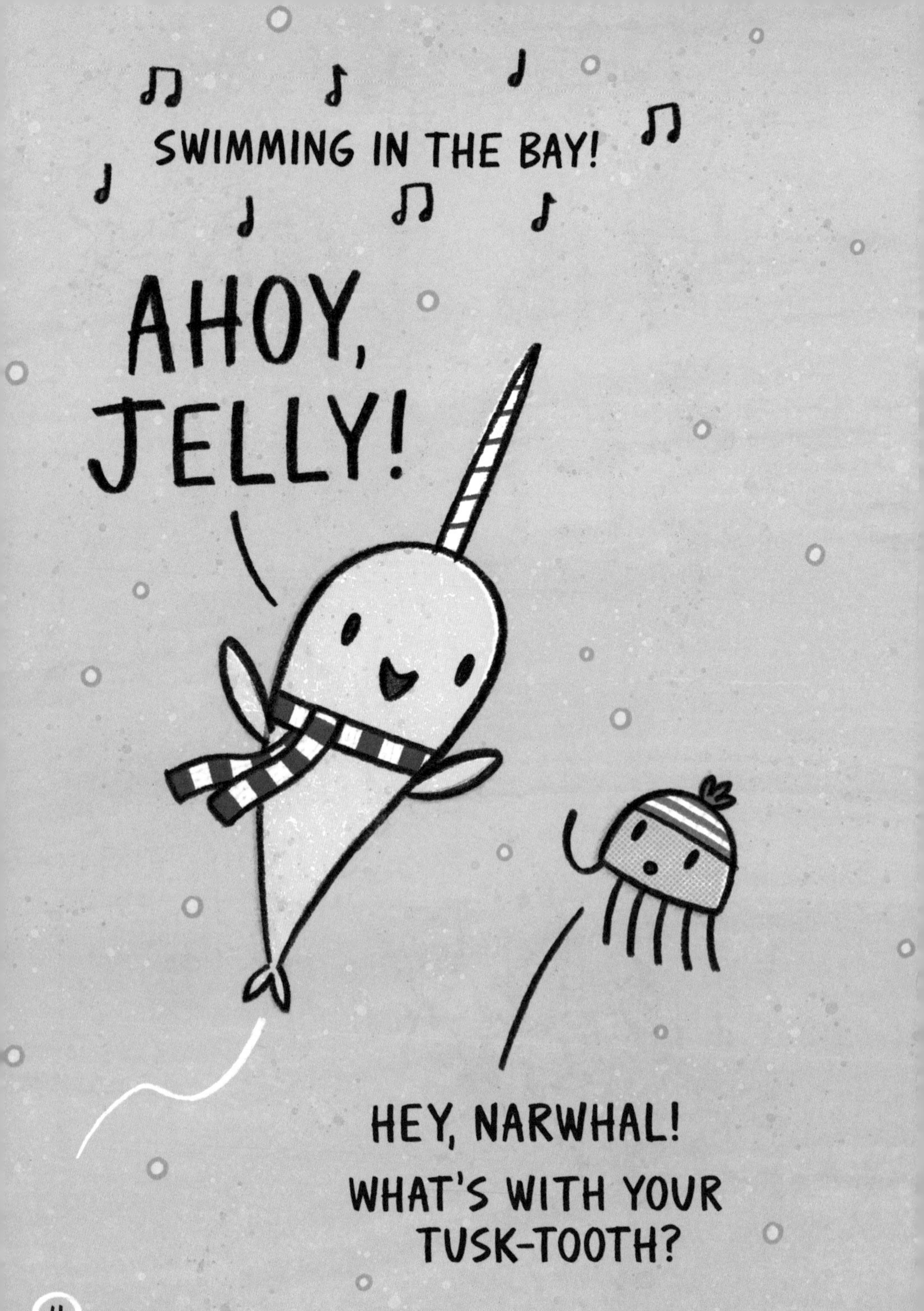
SWIMMING IN THE BAY!
AHOY, JELLY!
HEY, NARWHAL!
WHAT'S WITH YOUR TUSK-TOOTH?

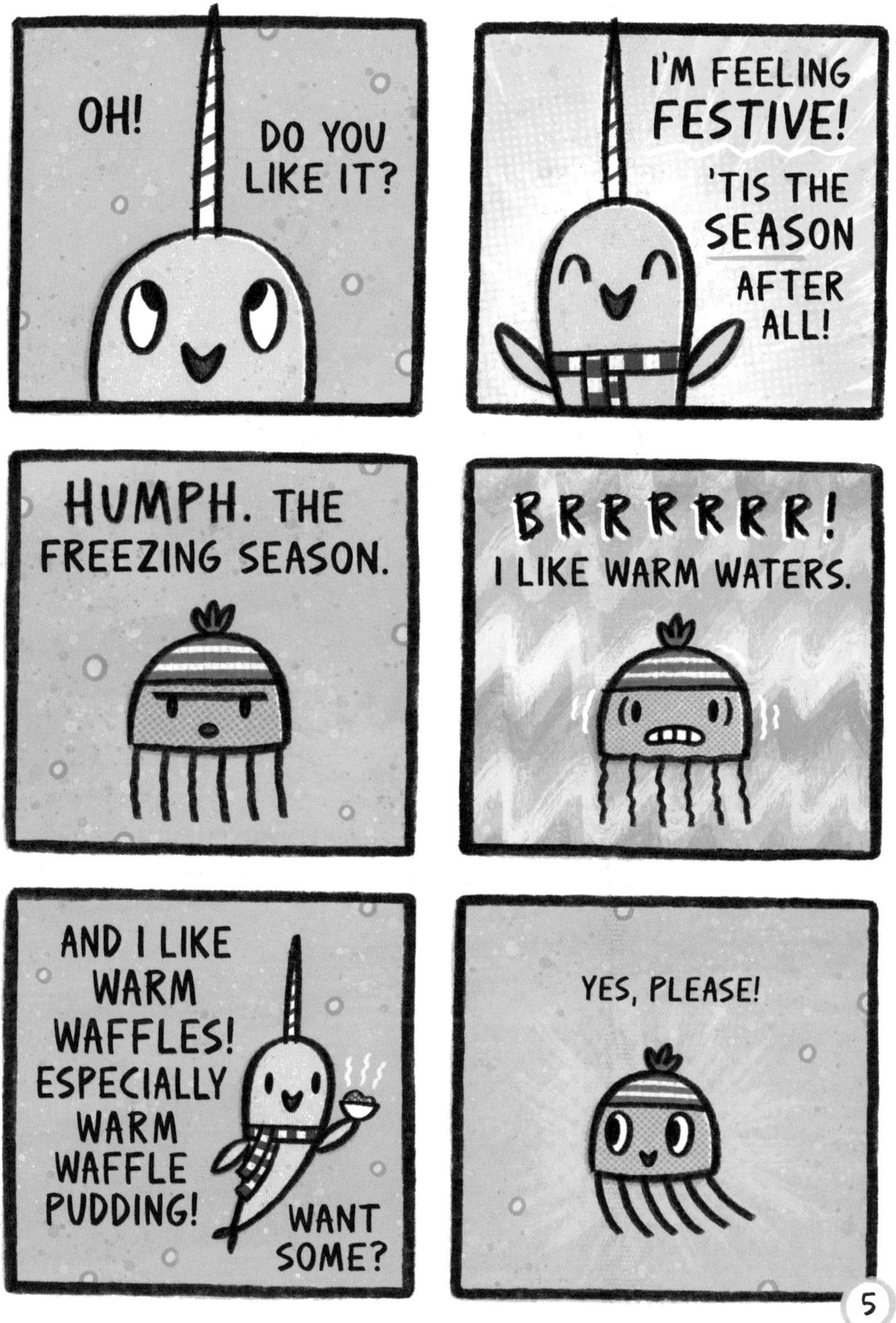

OH!
DO YOU LIKE IT?
I'M FEELING FESTIVE!
'TIS THE SEASON AFTER ALL!
HUMPH. THE FREEZING SEASON.
BRRRRRRR!
I LIKE WARM WATERS.
AND I LIKE WARM WAFFLES! ESPECIALLY WARM WAFFLE PUDDING!
WANT SOME?
YES, PLEASE!

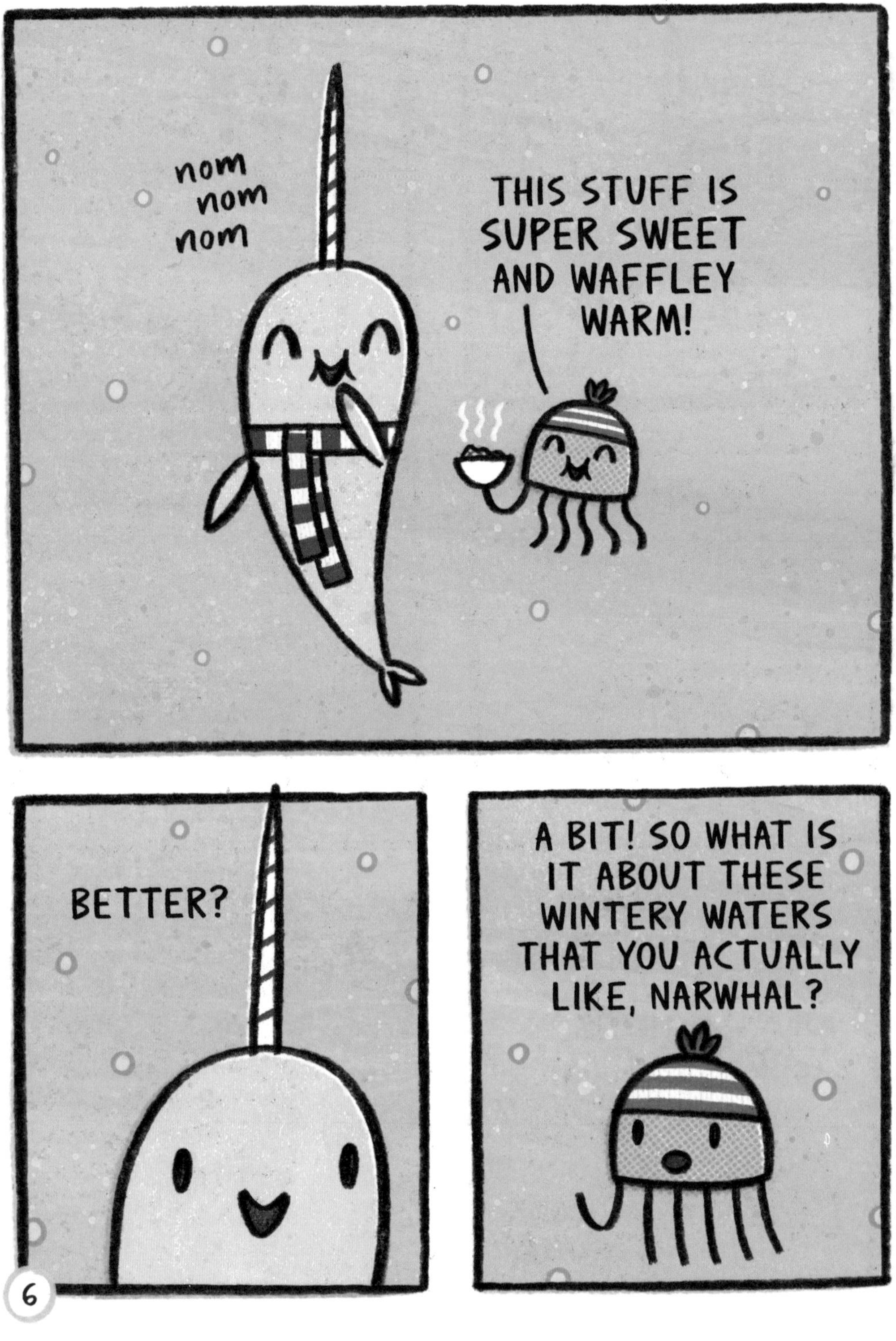
nom nom nom
THIS STUFF IS SUPER SWEET AND WAFFLEY WARM!
BETTER?
A BIT! SO WHAT IS IT ABOUT THESE WINTERY WATERS THAT YOU ACTUALLY LIKE, NARWHAL?

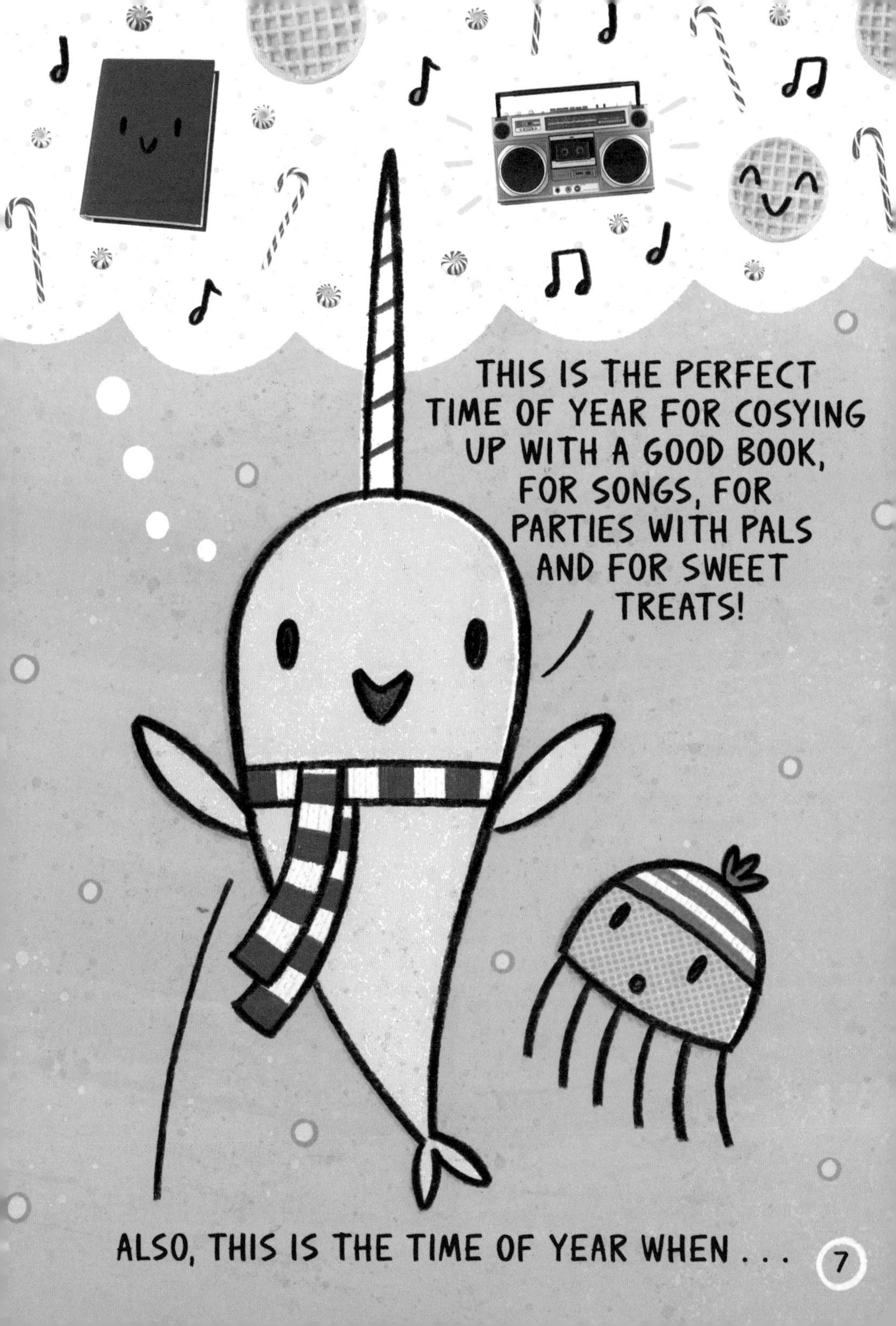
THIS IS THE PERFECT TIME OF YEAR FOR COSYING UP WITH A GOOD BOOK, FOR SONGS, FOR PARTIES WITH PALS AND FOR SWEET TREATS!
ALSO, THIS IS THE TIME OF YEAR WHEN . . .

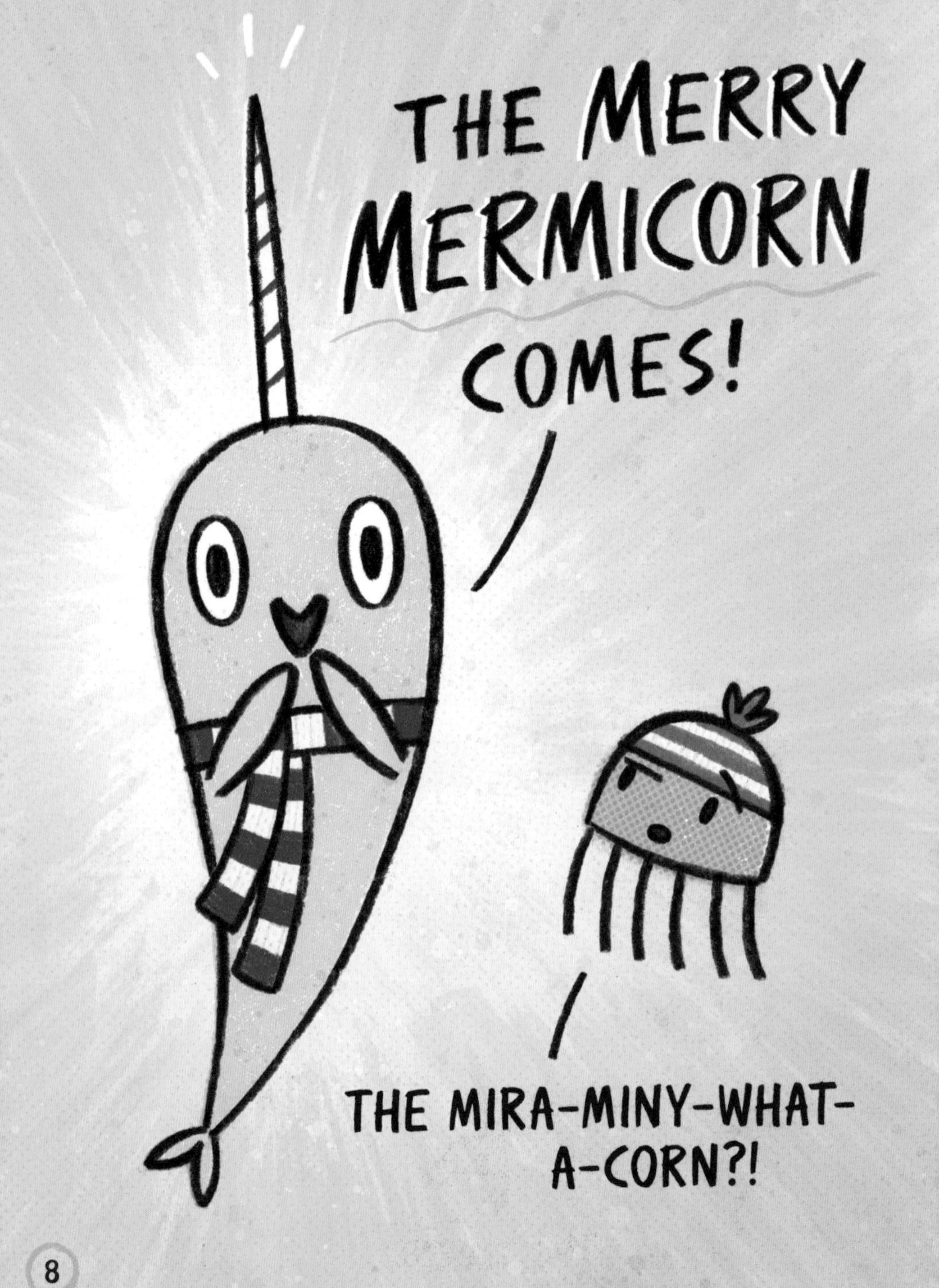
THE MERRY MERMICORN COMES!
THE MIRA-MINY-WHAT-A-CORN?!

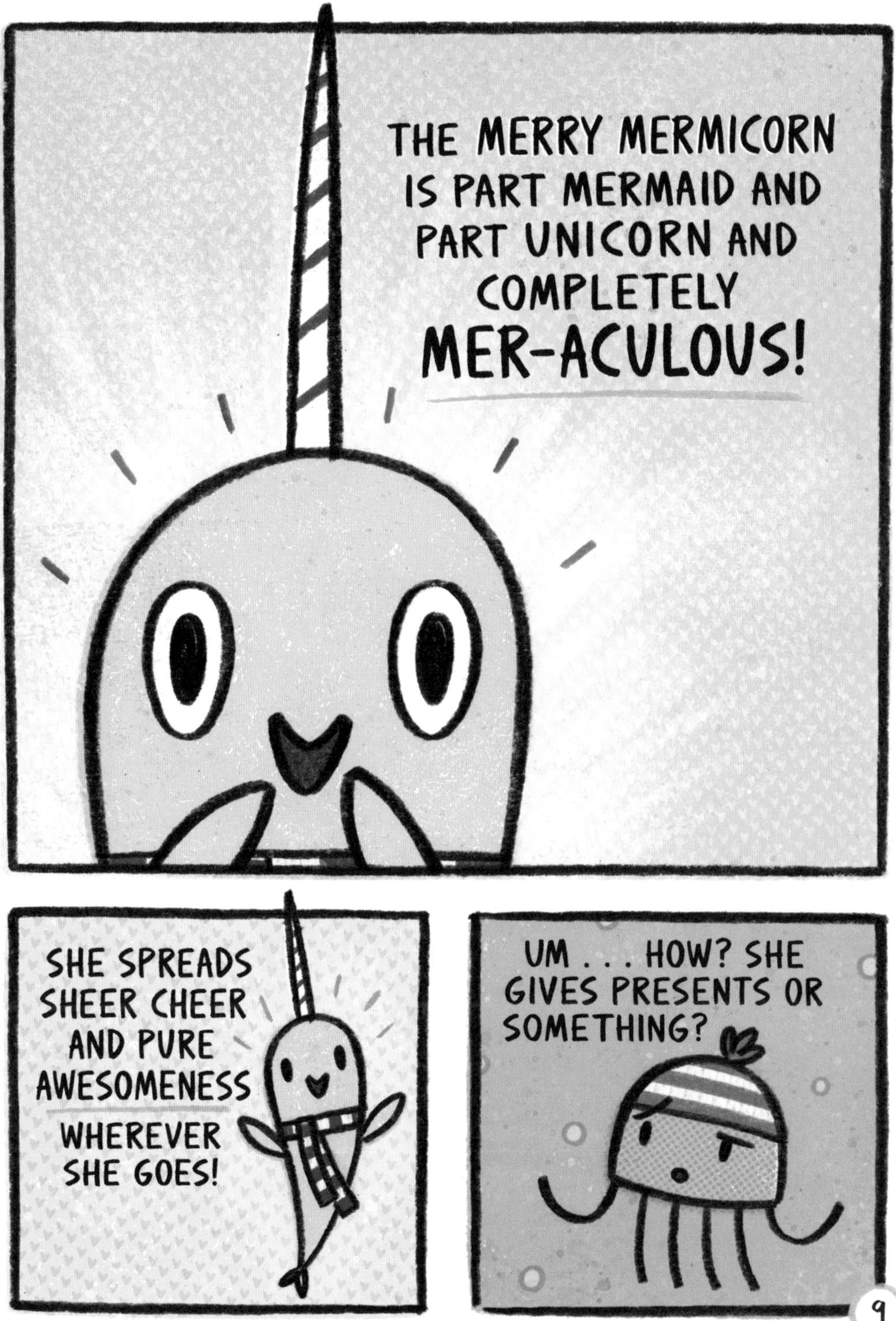
THE MERRY MERMICORN IS PART MERMAID AND PART UNICORN AND COMPLETELY MER-ACULOUS!
SHE SPREADS SHEER CHEER AND PURE AWESOMENESS WHEREVER SHE GOES!
UM . . . HOW? SHE GIVES PRESENTS OR SOMETHING?

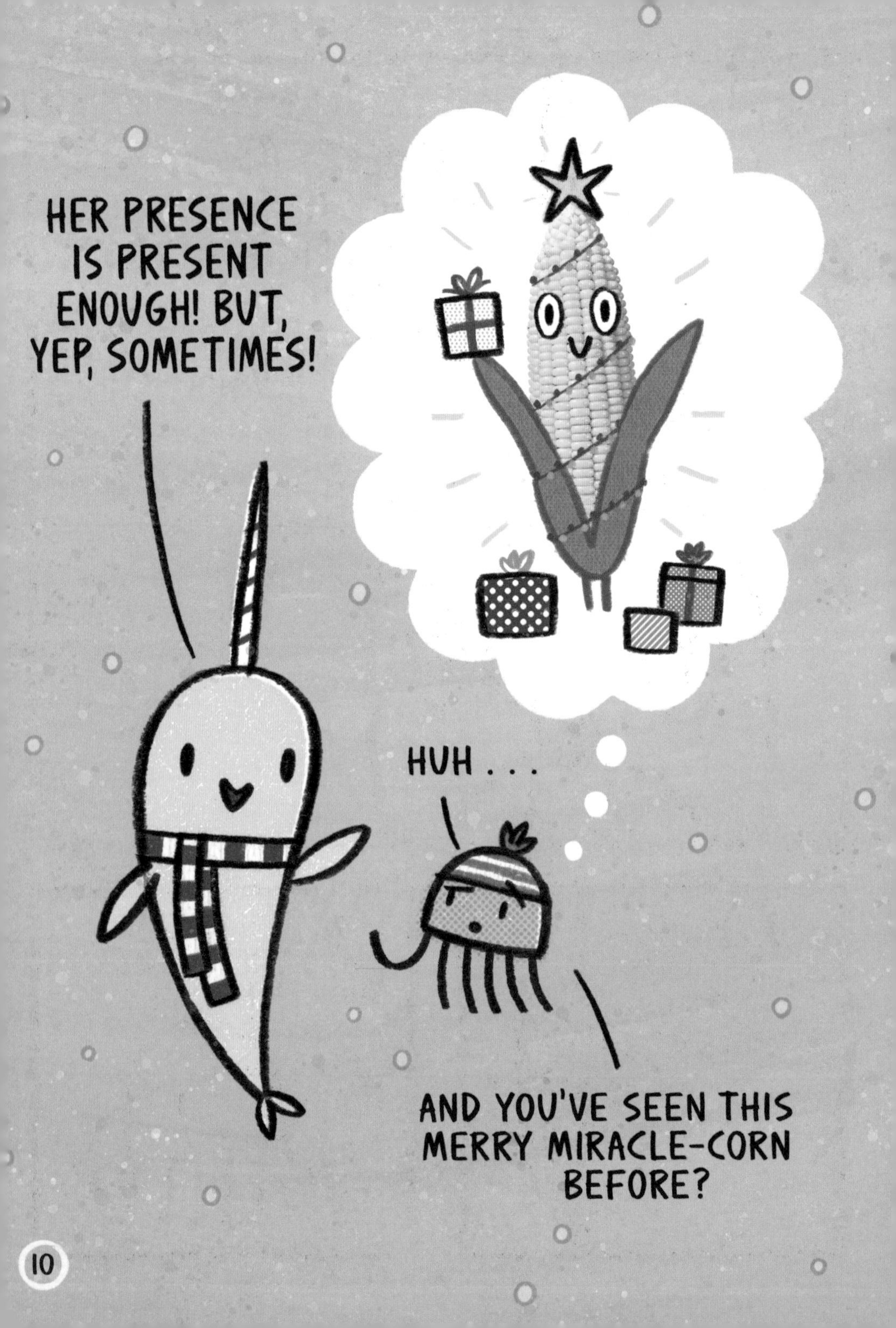
HER PRESENCE IS PRESENT ENOUGH! BUT, YEP, SOMETIMES!
HUH . . .
AND YOU'VE SEEN THIS MERRY MIRACLE-CORN BEFORE?

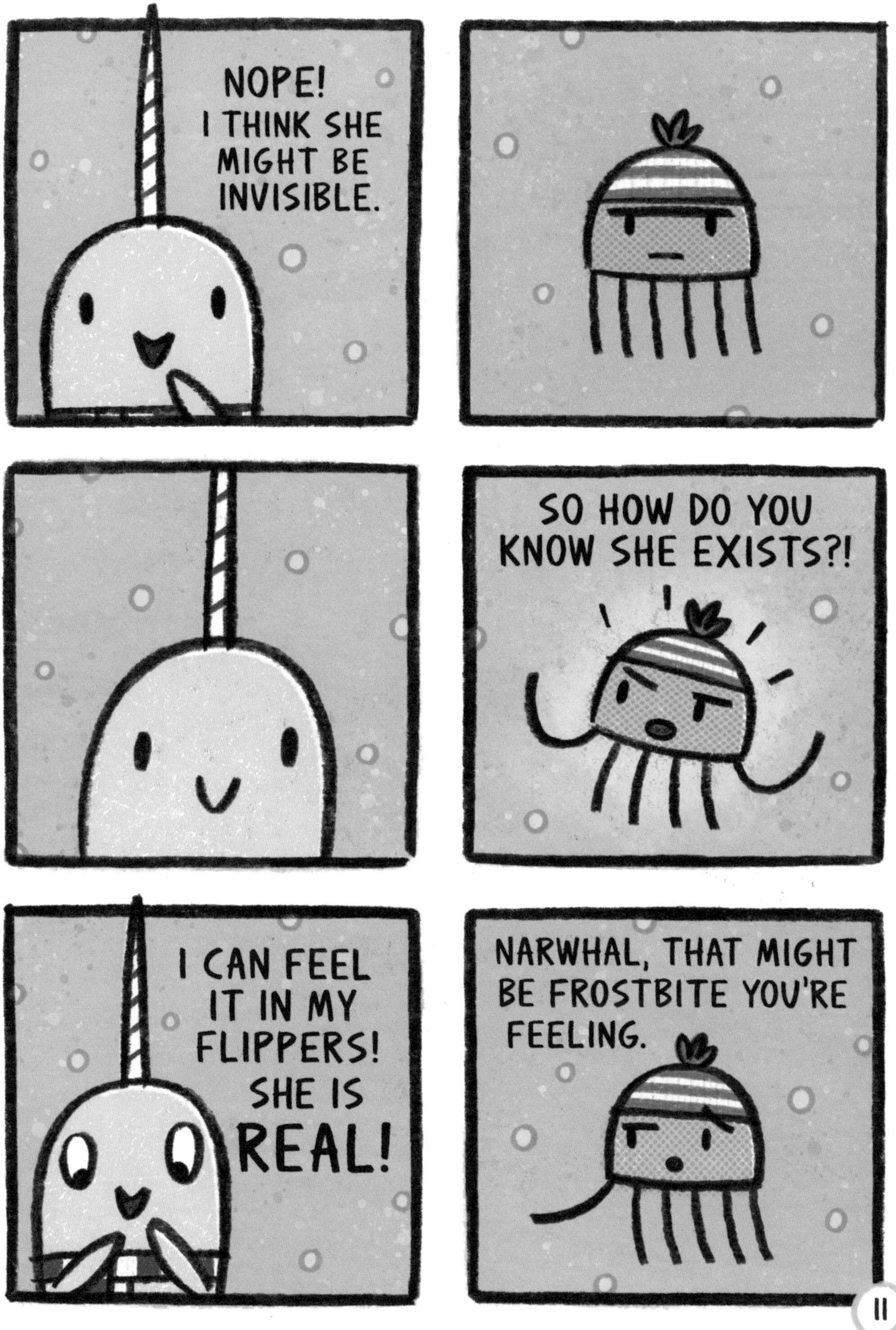
NOPE! I THINK SHE MIGHT BE INVISIBLE.
SO HOW DO YOU KNOW SHE EXISTS?!
I CAN FEEL IT IN MY FLIPPERS! SHE IS REAL!
NARWHAL, THAT MIGHT BE FROSTBITE YOU'RE FEELING.

DO YOU REMEMBER WHEN WE MET? HOW I THOUGHT **YOU** WERE IMAGINARY?

YEP! AND I THOUGHT YOU MUST BE MY IMAGINARY FRIEND!

RIGHT. SINCE THEN IT'S BECOME PRETTY CLEAR YOU'RE ACTUALLY REAL. SHARK SEES YOU. TURTLE SEES YOU. MR. BLOWFISH . . . EVERYONE! SO UNLESS EVERYONE ELSE IS ALSO IMAGINING YOU, OR I'M IMAGINING EVERYONE ELSE IS IMAGINING YOU, YOU **ARE** REAL.

THIS MERRY CORN . . . NOT SO MUCH.
NOT A CHANCE!

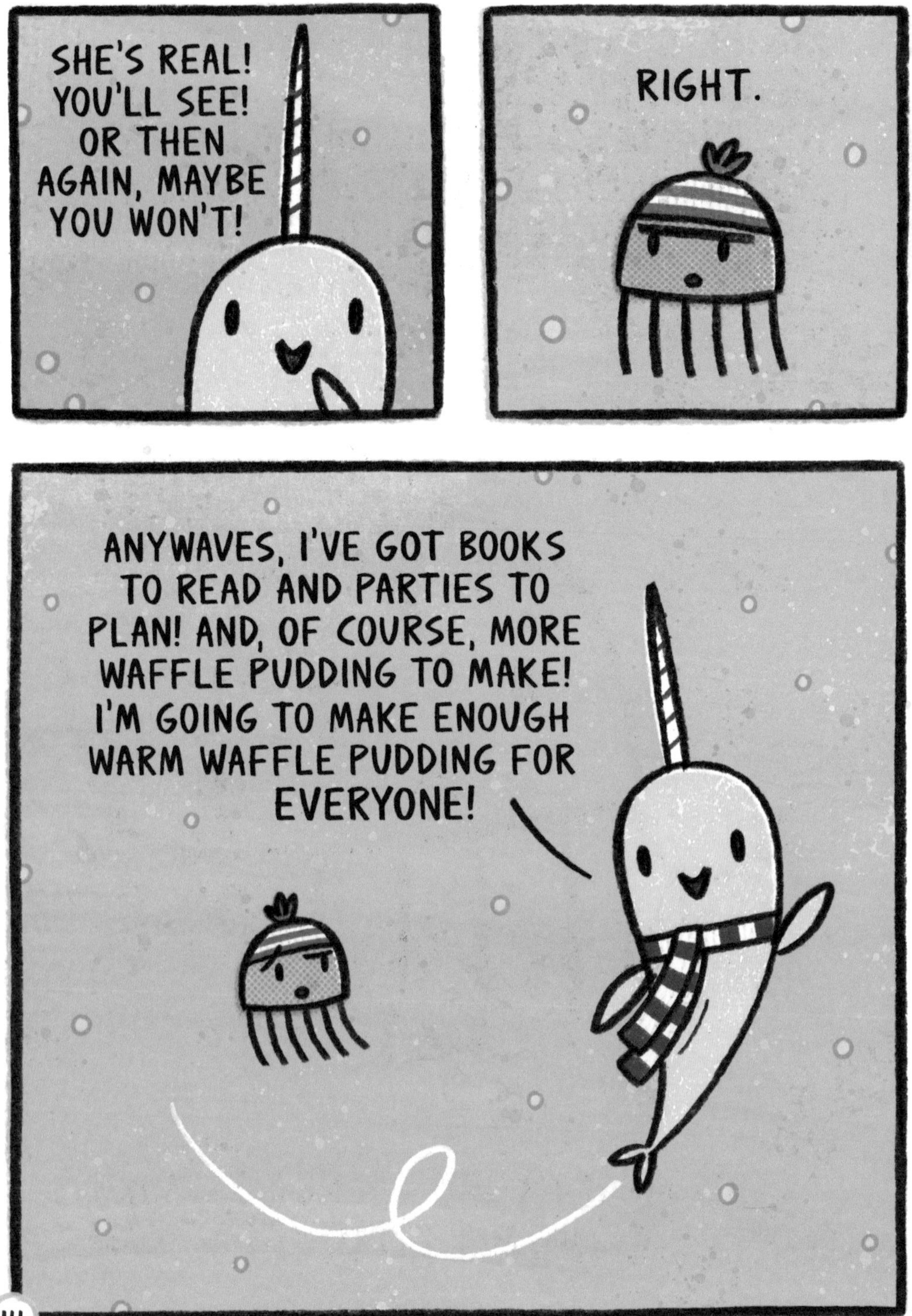
SHE'S REAL! YOU'LL SEE! OR THEN AGAIN, MAYBE YOU WON'T!
RIGHT.
ANYWAVES, I'VE GOT BOOKS TO READ AND PARTIES TO PLAN! AND, OF COURSE, MORE WAFFLE PUDDING TO MAKE! I'M GOING TO MAKE ENOUGH WARM WAFFLE PUDDING FOR EVERYONE!

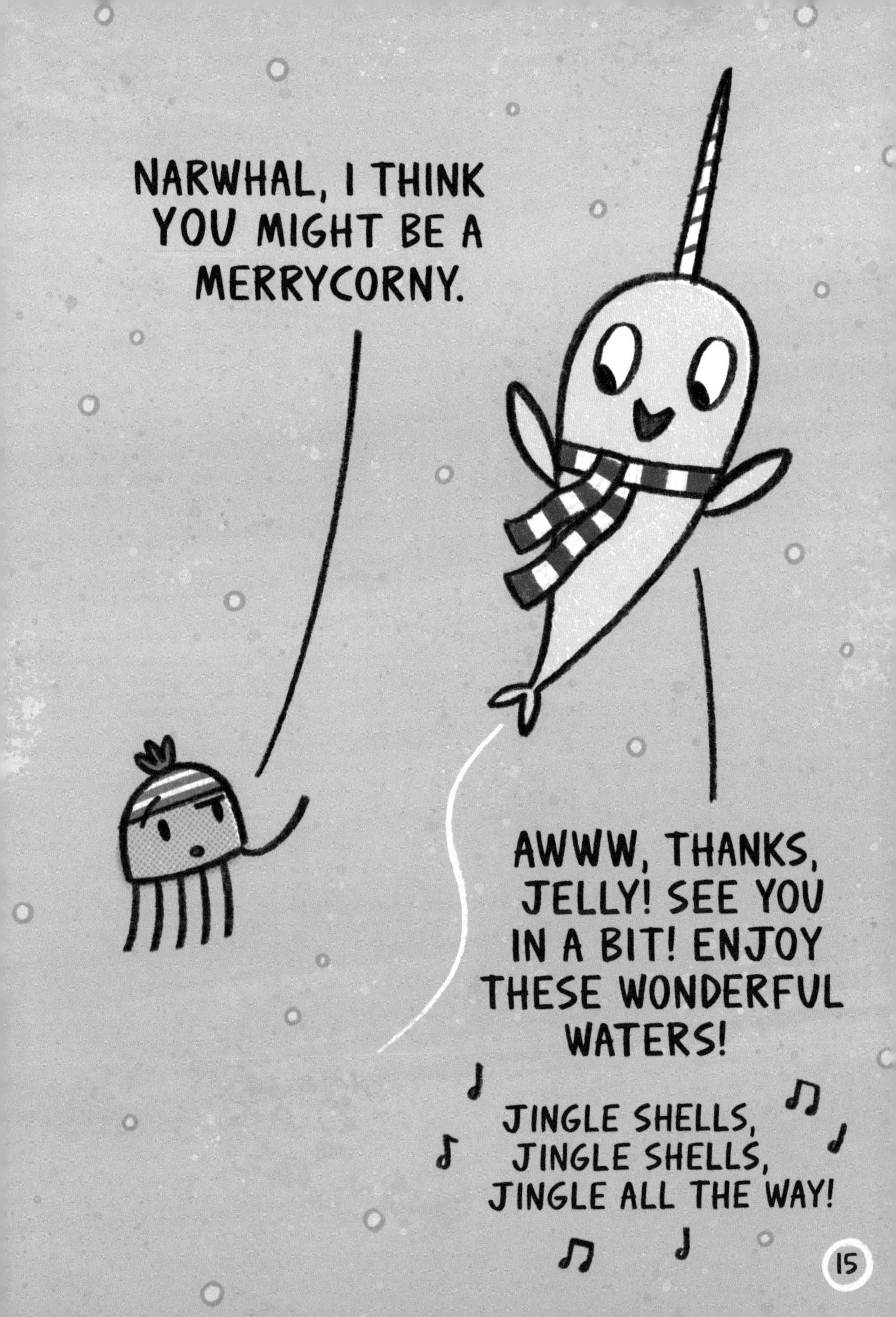
NARWHAL, I THINK YOU MIGHT BE A MERRYCORNY.
AWWW, THANKS, JELLY! SEE YOU IN A BIT! ENJOY THESE WONDERFUL WATERS!
JINGLE SHELLS, JINGLE SHELLS, JINGLE ALL THE WAY!

HUMPH-BUG.

COOL FACTS

NARWHALS LIVE IN THE COLD ARCTIC OCEAN. A FATTY TISSUE CALLED BLUBBER KEEPS THEM WARM. BLUBBER MAKES UP MORE THAN A THIRD OF A NARWHAL'S WEIGHT.

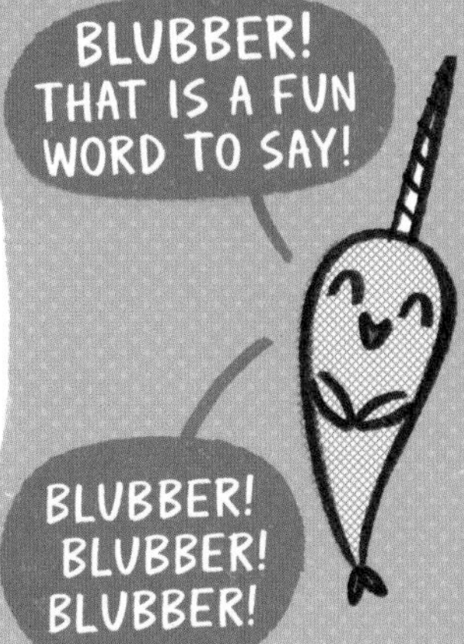
BLUBBER! THAT IS A FUN WORD TO SAY!
BLUBBER! BLUBBER! BLUBBER!

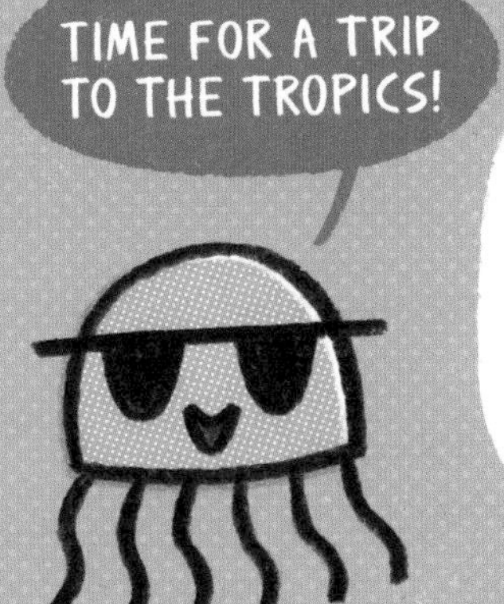
TIME FOR A TRIP TO THE TROPICS!

JELLYFISH CAN BE FOUND IN ALL SORTS OF WATERS. SOME LIVE IN THE COLD ARCTIC WATERS AND OTHERS LIVE IN WARM TROPICAL WATERS.

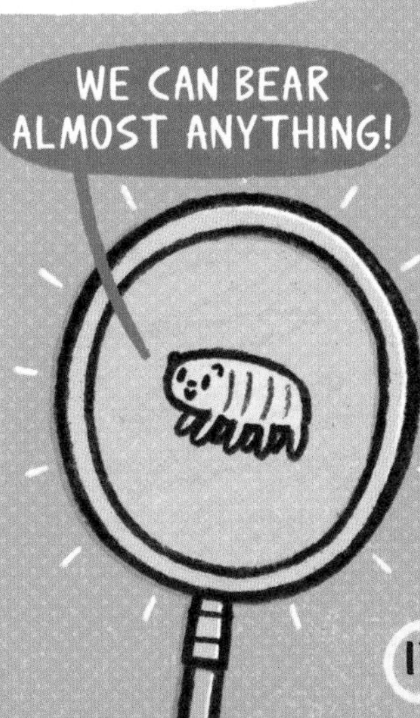
WE CAN BEAR ALMOST ANYTHING!

TARDIGRADES, COMMONLY KNOWN AS WATER BEARS, ARE WATER-DWELLING MICRO-ANIMALS THAT CAN SURVIVE IN TEMPERATURES AS HOT AS 304°F (151°C) AND AS COLD AS ABSOLUTE ZERO.

MORE COOL FACTS

NICE!

SNOW UNDERWATER? MARINE SNOW IS ACTUALLY A SHOWER OF MOSTLY ORGANIC MATERIAL FALLING FROM THE UPPER WATERS OF THE OCEAN.

GREENLAND SHARKS, WHICH CAN LIVE FOR POSSIBLY 400 YEARS, PREFER COLD WATERS. DURING WINTER, THEY MIGRATE TO THE SURFACE LAYER, WHICH IS COLDER THAN THE SEA FLOOR AT THAT TIME OF YEAR.

WE'RE COLD-BLOODED!

CUDDLE-HUDDLE TIME!

EMPEROR PENGUINS HUDDLE TOGETHER TO KEEP FROM FREEZING.

DENSE, LAYERED FEATHERS AND INSULATING FAT ARE VITAL TO PENGUINS' SURVIVAL.

THE
PERFECT
PRESENT

A LITTLE WHILE LATER, WHEN TRYING TO FIND SOME WARMER WATERS . . .

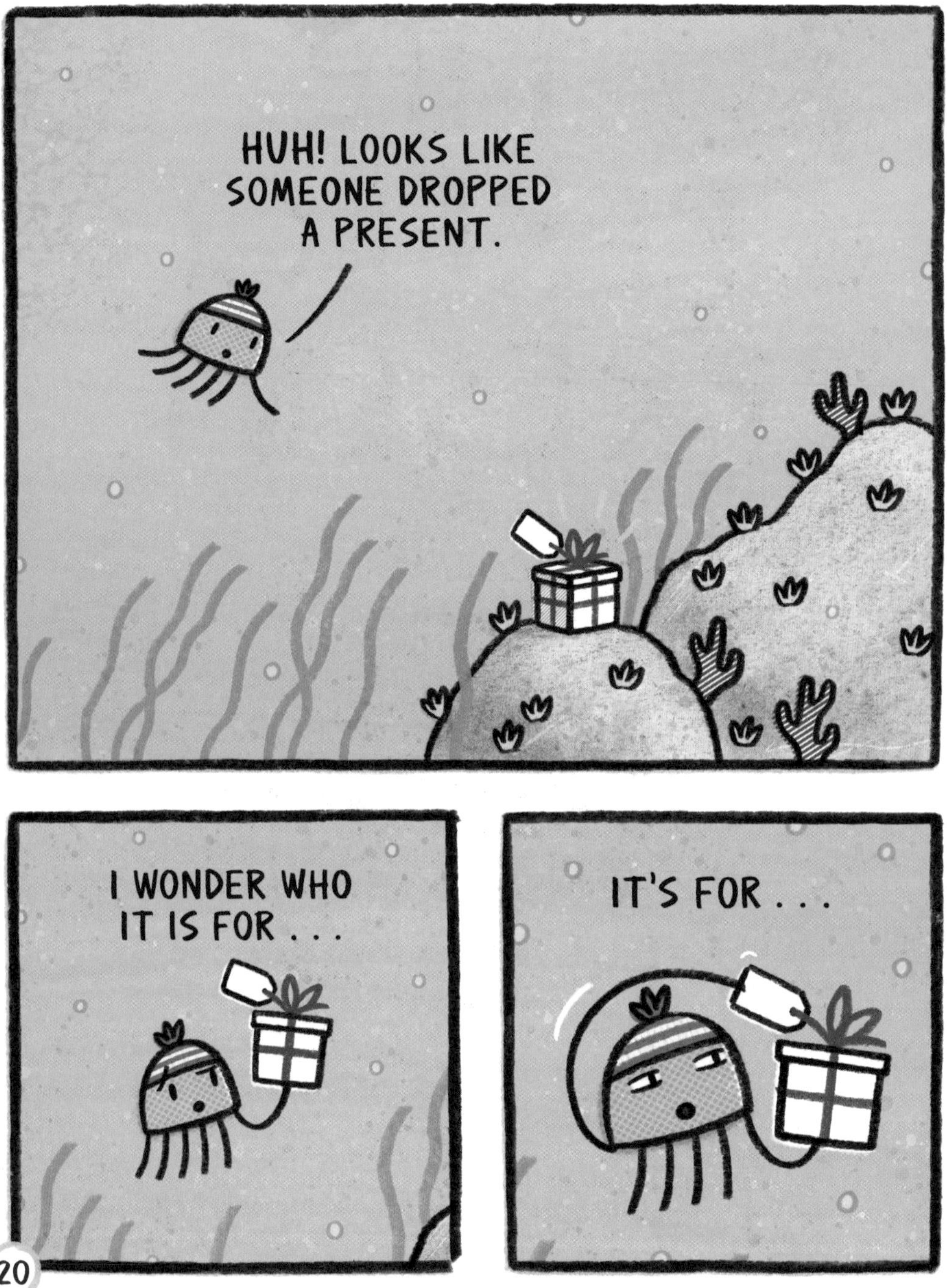

HUH! LOOKS LIKE SOMEONE DROPPED A PRESENT.
I WONDER WHO IT IS FOR . . .
IT'S FOR . . .

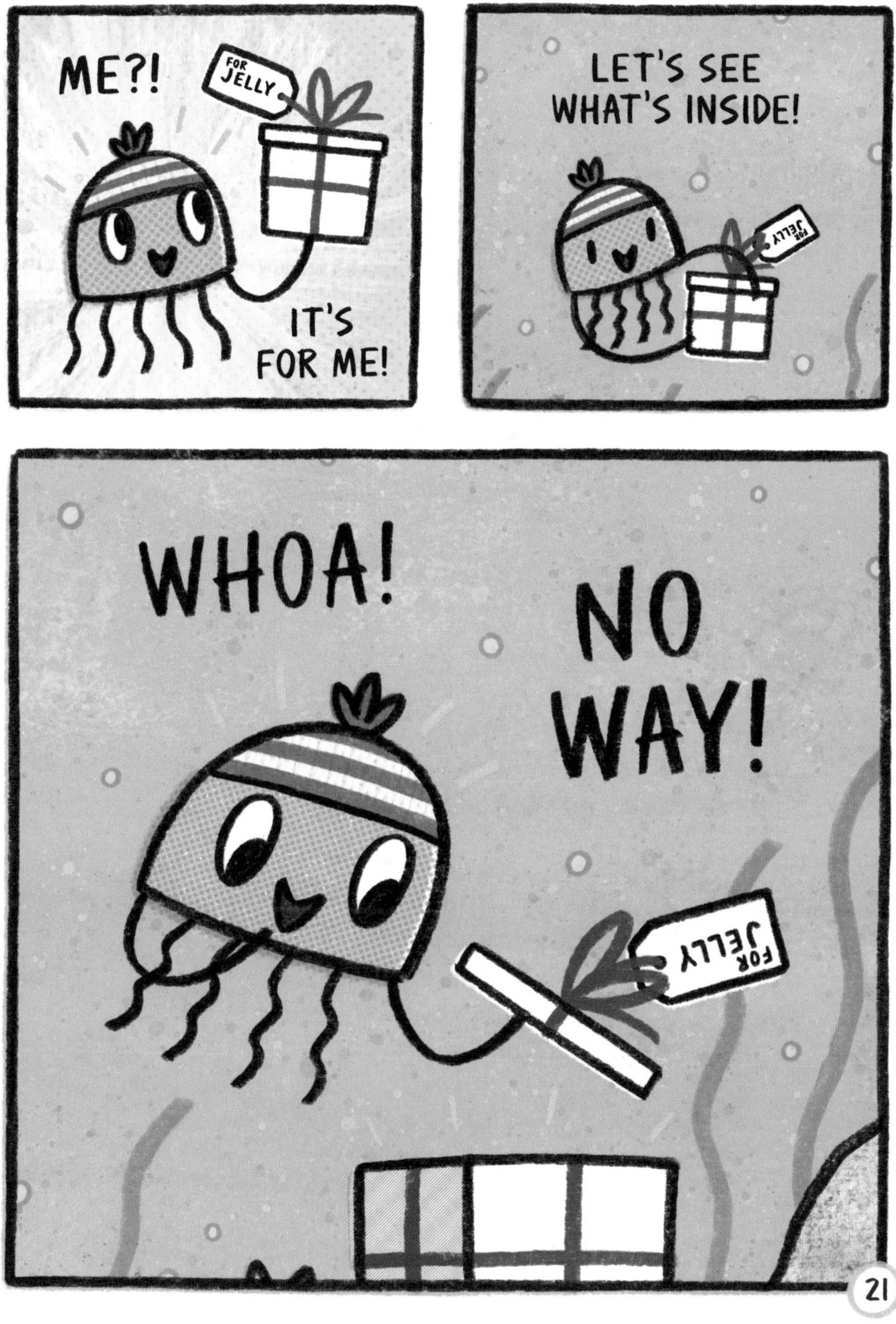
ME?!
FOR JELLY
IT'S FOR ME!
LET'S SEE WHAT'S INSIDE!
FOR JELLY
WHOA!
NO WAY!
FOR JELLY

MITTENS!

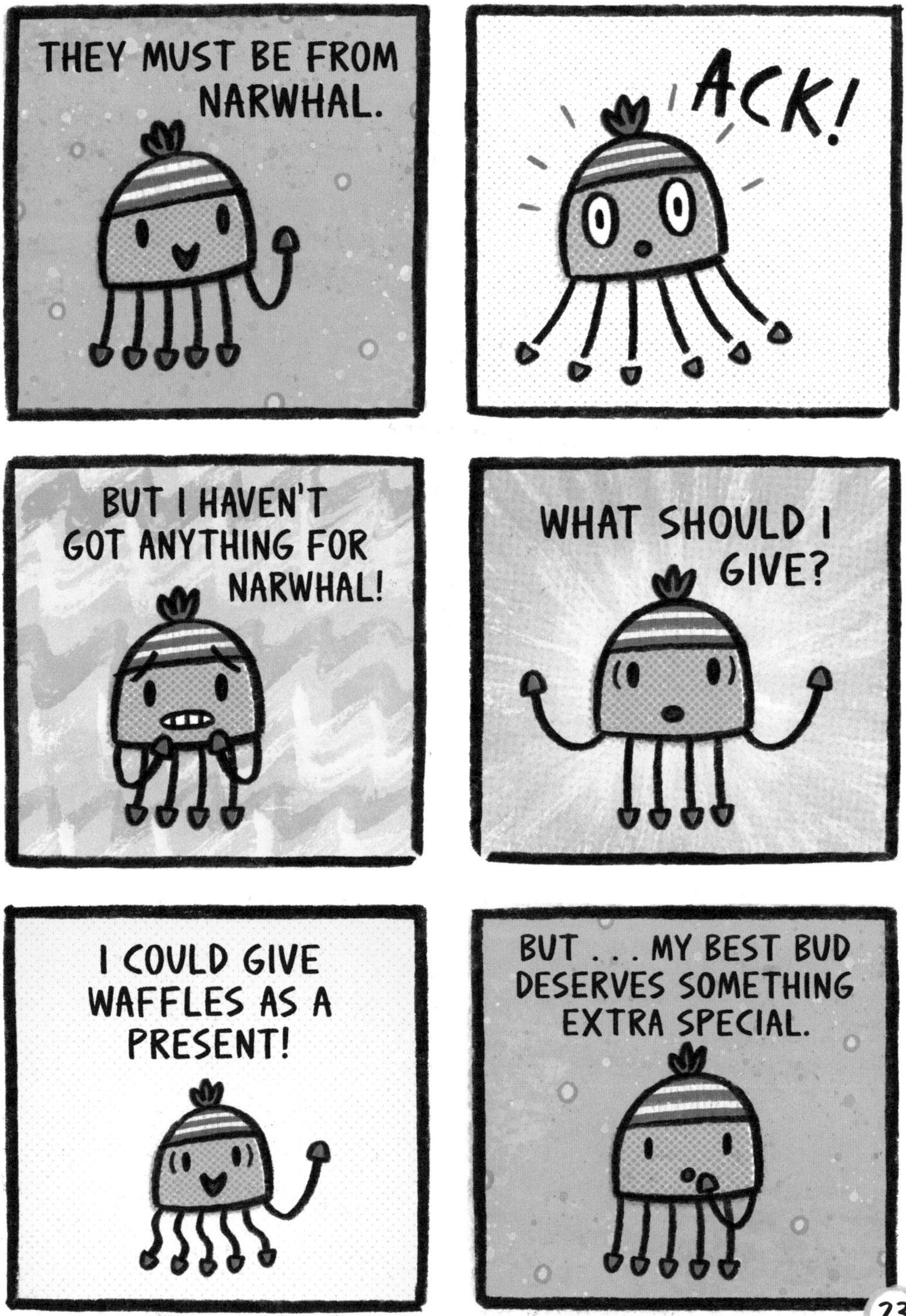
THEY MUST BE FROM NARWHAL.
ACK!
BUT I HAVEN'T GOT ANYTHING FOR NARWHAL!
WHAT SHOULD I GIVE?
I COULD GIVE WAFFLES AS A PRESENT!
BUT . . . MY BEST BUD DESERVES SOMETHING EXTRA SPECIAL.

SOMETHING AS
SUPER AND UNIQUE
AS NARWHAL!

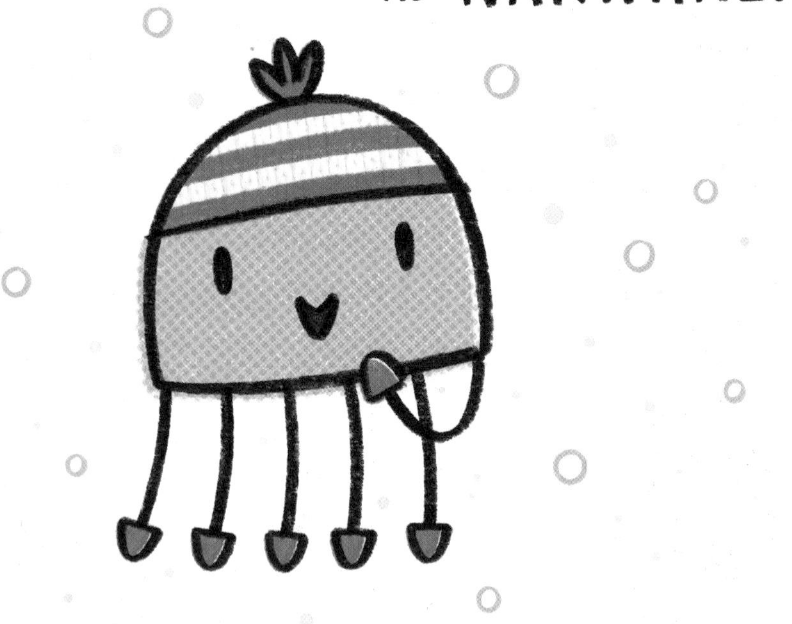

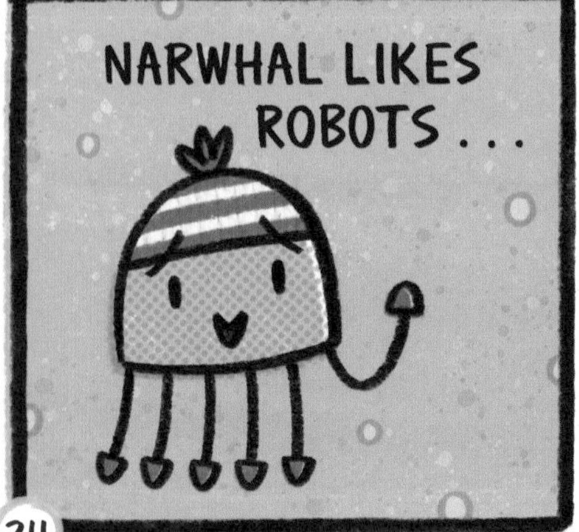
NARWHAL LIKES ROBOTS . . .

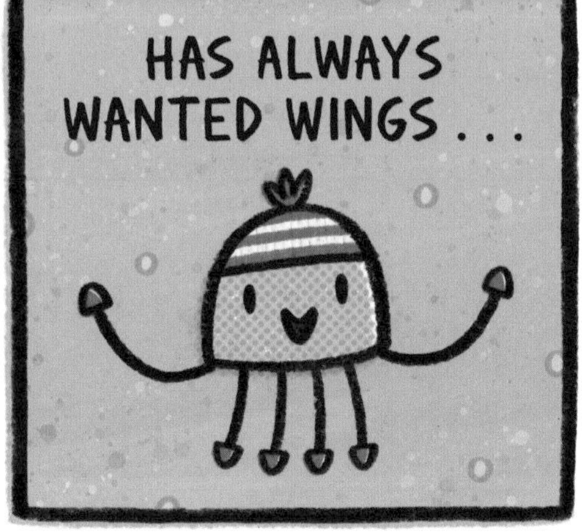
HAS ALWAYS WANTED WINGS . . .

AND LOVES
POLKA DOTS!

HOW ABOUT . . .

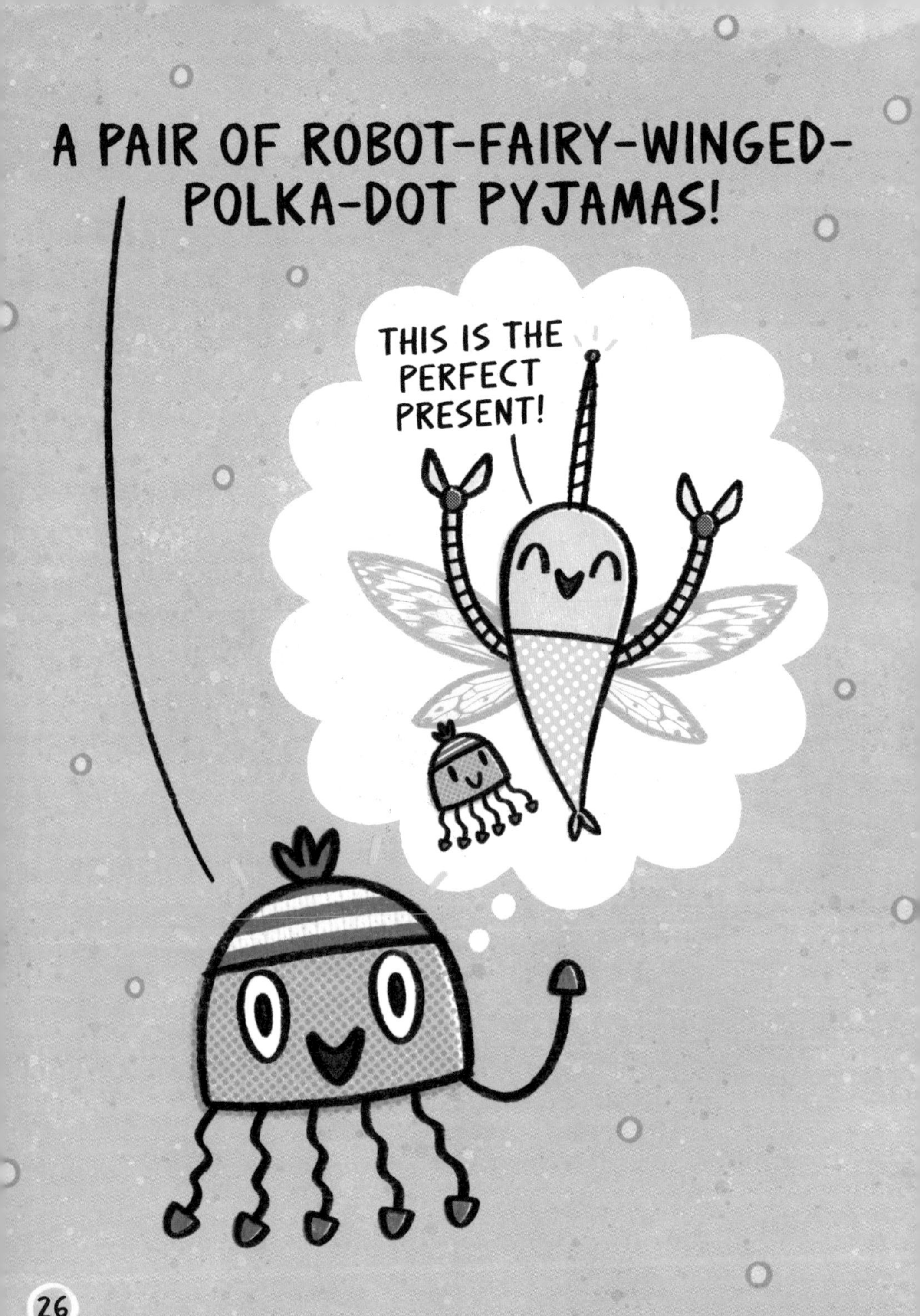
A PAIR OF ROBOT-FAIRY-WINGED-POLKA-DOT PYJAMAS!
THIS IS THE PERFECT PRESENT!

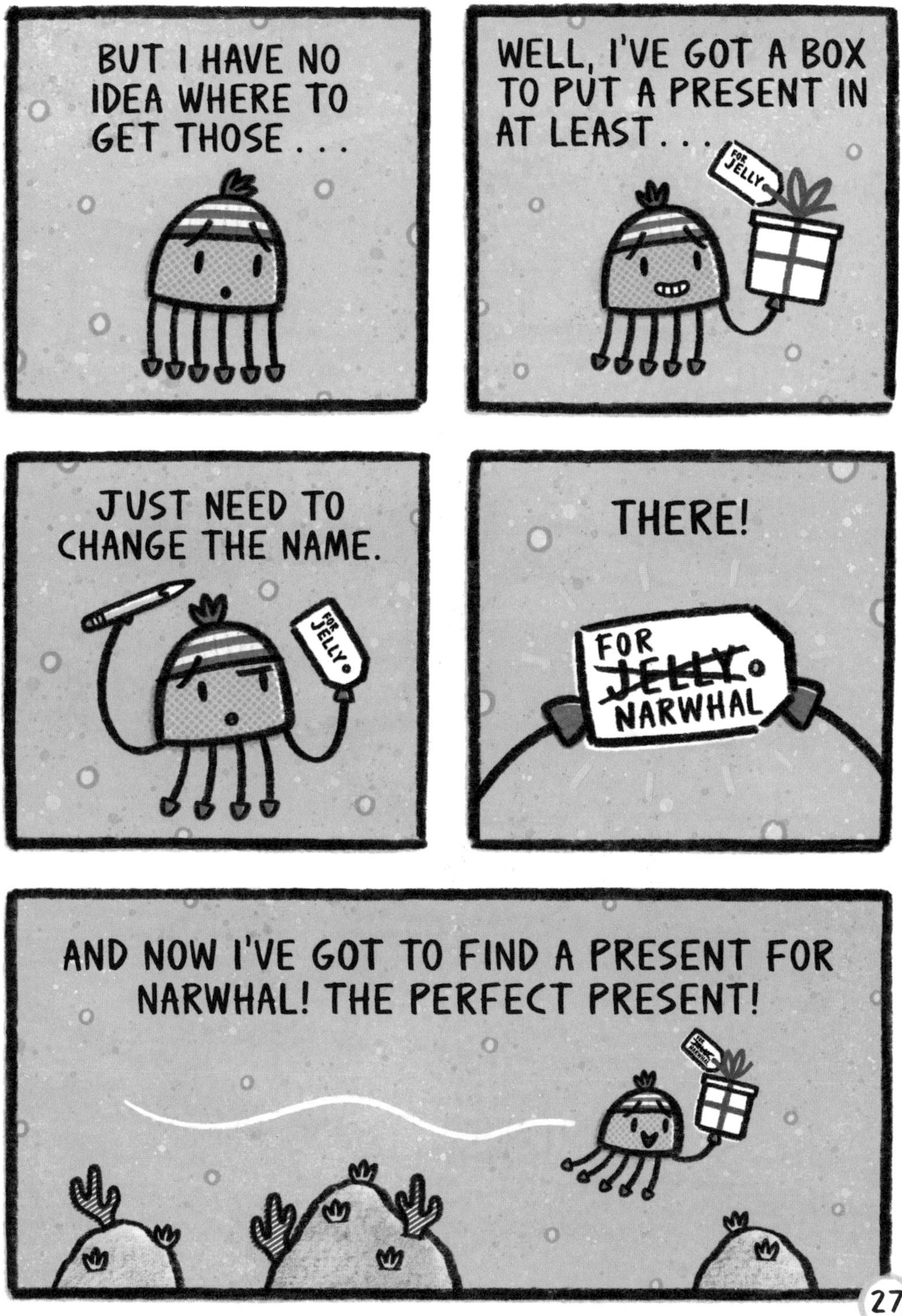
BUT I HAVE NO IDEA WHERE TO GET THOSE . . .
WELL, I'VE GOT A BOX TO PUT A PRESENT IN AT LEAST . . .
FOR JELLY
JUST NEED TO CHANGE THE NAME.
FOR JELLY
THERE!
FOR JELLY NARWHAL
AND NOW I'VE GOT TO FIND A PRESENT FOR NARWHAL! THE PERFECT PRESENT!

3 HOURS, 41 MINUTES AND 17 SECONDS LATER . . .

FINDING THE PERFECT PRESENT IS PRETTY TOUGH.

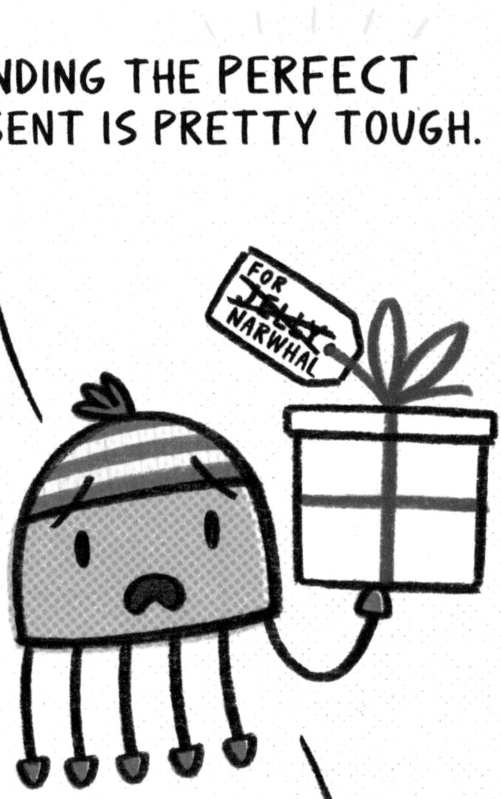
FOR ~~JELLY~~ NARWHAL

MAYBE I NEED SOME HELP . . .

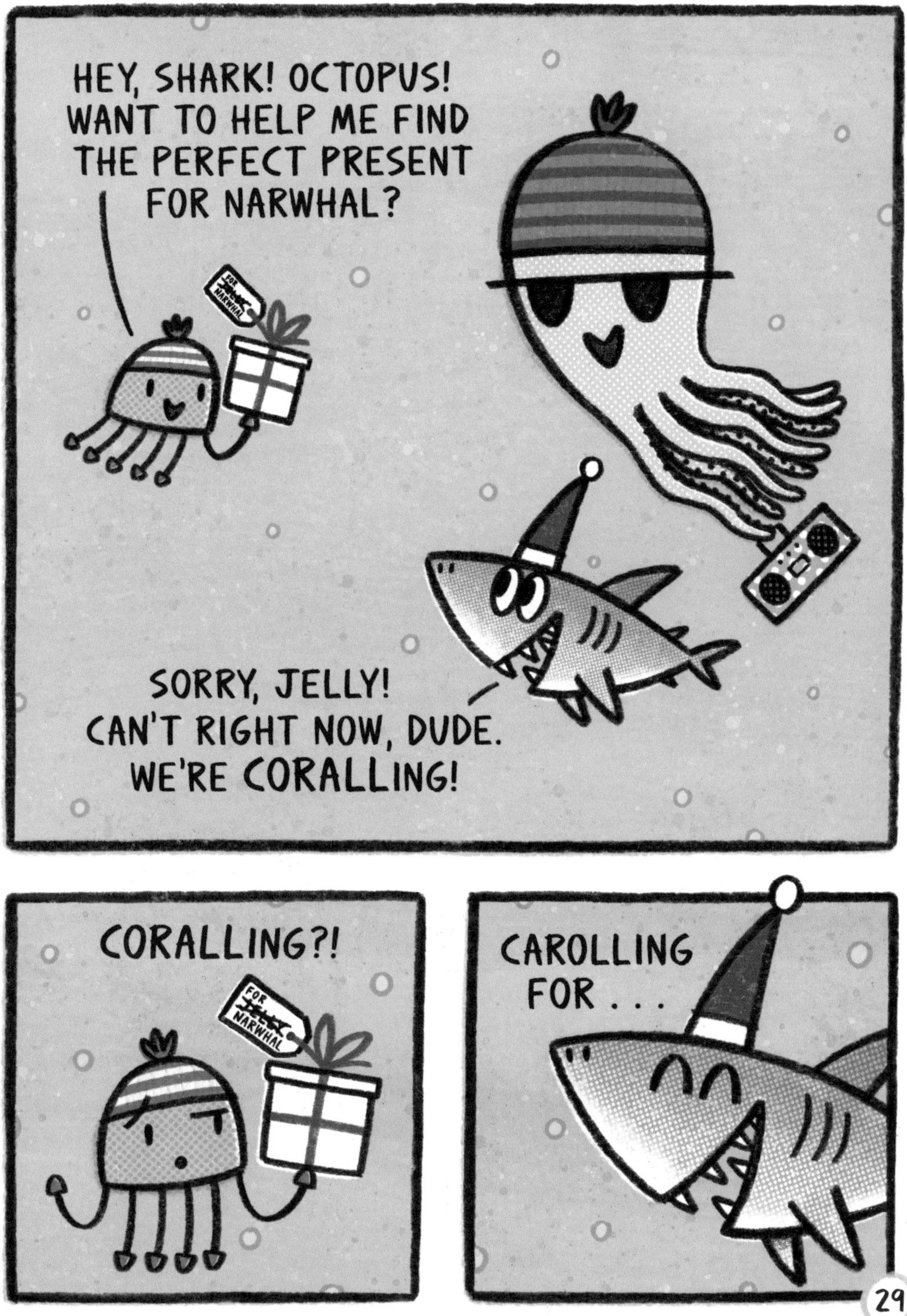
HEY, SHARK! OCTOPUS! WANT TO HELP ME FIND THE PERFECT PRESENT FOR NARWHAL?
FOR NARWHAL
SORRY, JELLY! CAN'T RIGHT NOW, DUDE. WE'RE CORALLING!
CORALLING?!
FOR NARWHAL
CAROLLING FOR . . .

CORAL!

FOLLOW ME IN MERRY MEASURE,
FA-LA-LA-LA-LA, LA-LA-LA-LA!
WHILE I TELL OF YULETIDE TREASURE,
FA-LA-LA-LA-LA, LA-LA-LA-LA!

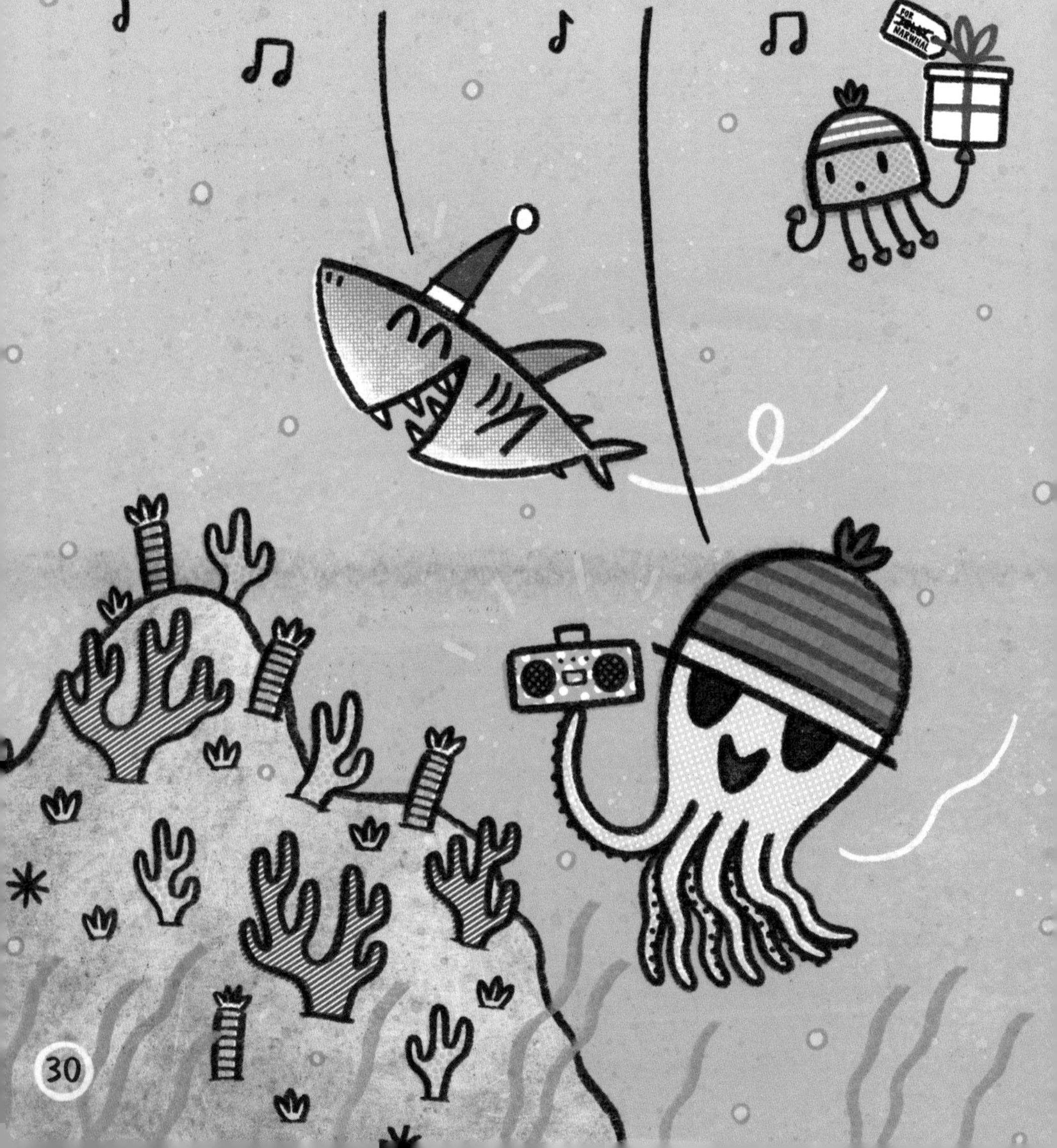

HEY, TURTLE AND SHELLY! CAN YOU HELP ME FIND THE PERFECT PRESENT FOR NARWHAL?

MAYBE LATER?

WE'RE OFF TO LIGHT THE MINNOW-ORAH!

LIGHT? HOW? WE'RE UNDERWATER.

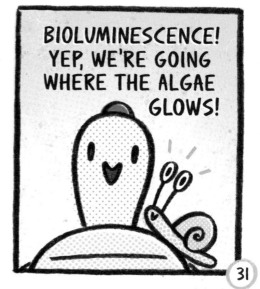

BIOLUMINESCENCE! YEP, WE'RE GOING WHERE THE ALGAE GLOWS!

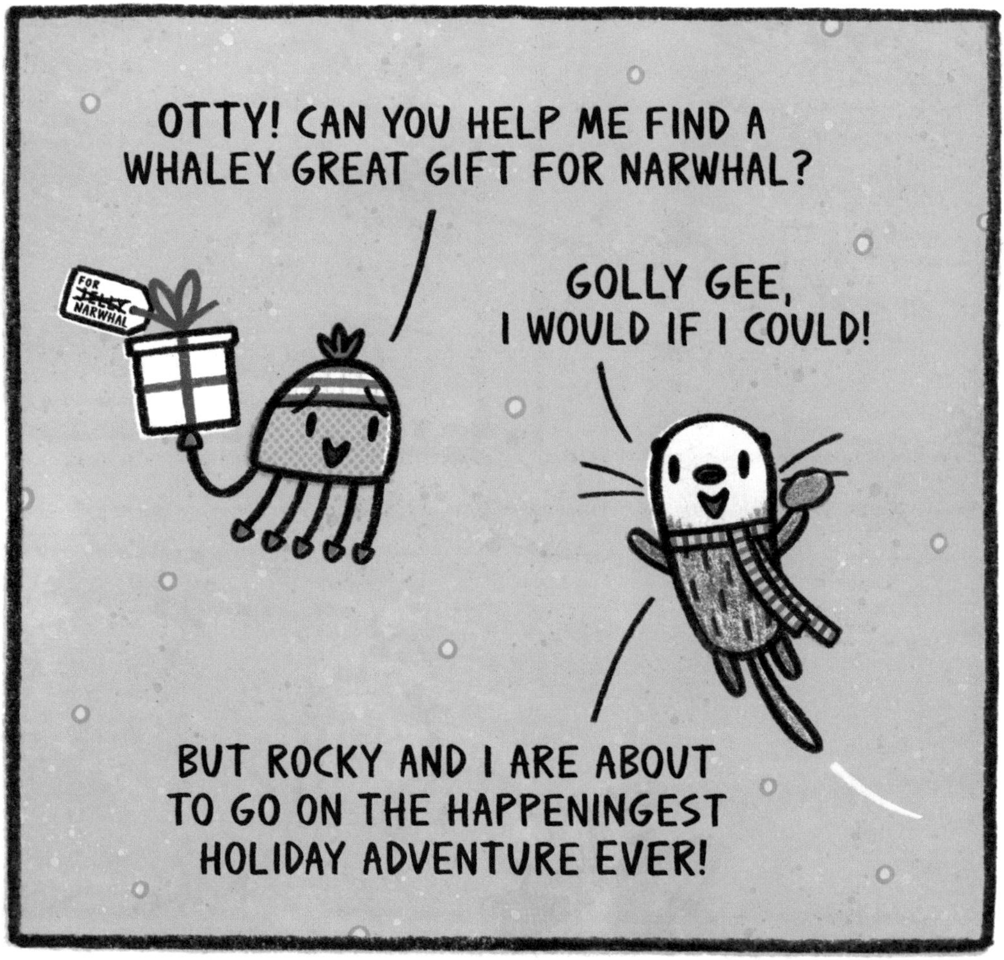
FOR
NARWHAL
OTTY! CAN YOU HELP ME FIND A WHALEY GREAT GIFT FOR NARWHAL?
GOLLY GEE, I WOULD IF I COULD!
BUT ROCKY AND I ARE ABOUT TO GO ON THE HAPPENINGEST HOLIDAY ADVENTURE EVER!

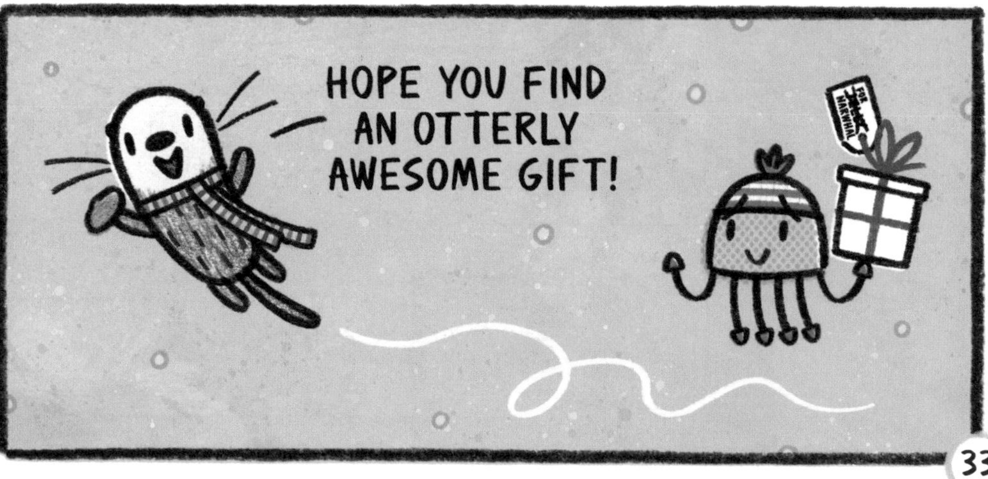
HOPE YOU FIND AN OTTERLY AWESOME GIFT!

35

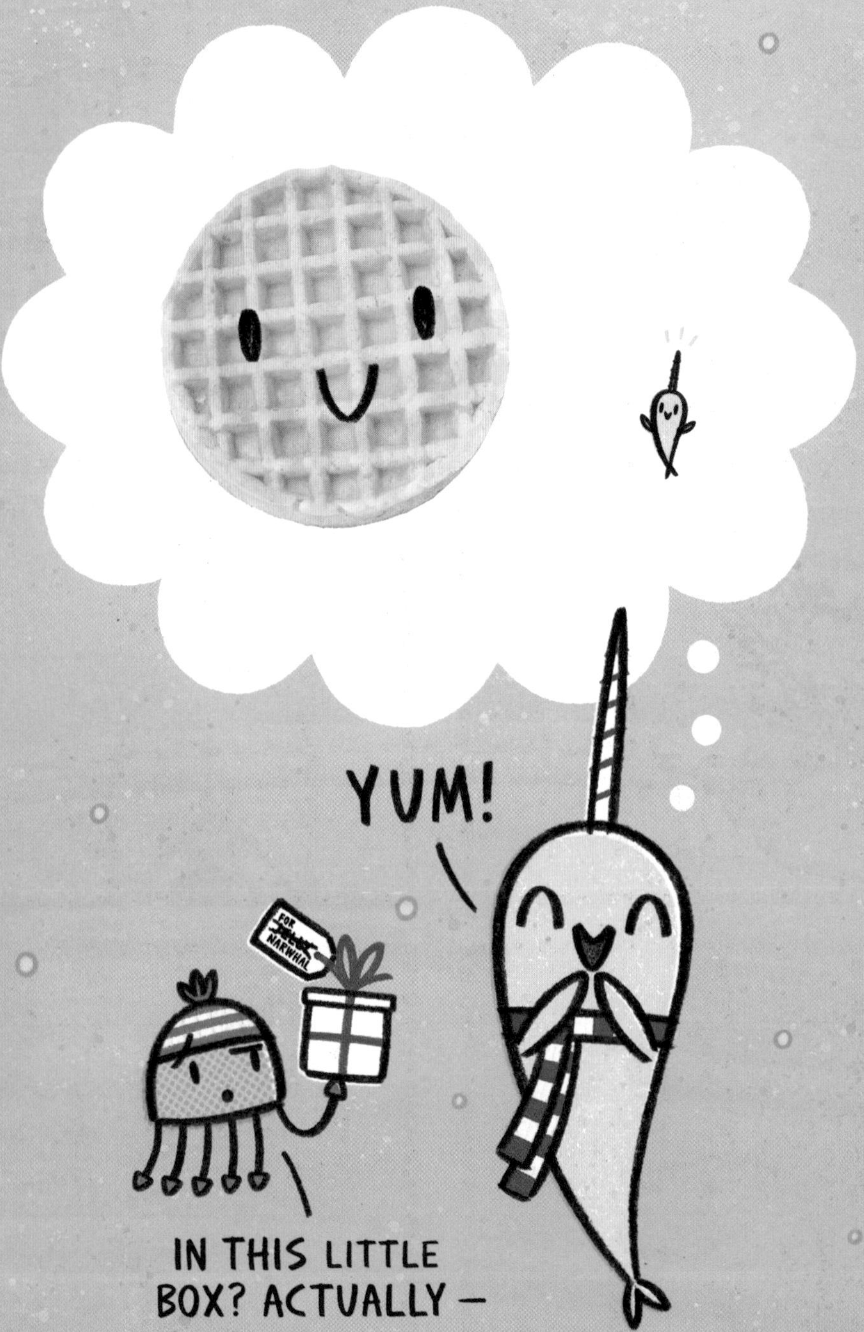
FOR
NARWHAL
YUM!
IN THIS LITTLE
BOX? ACTUALLY –

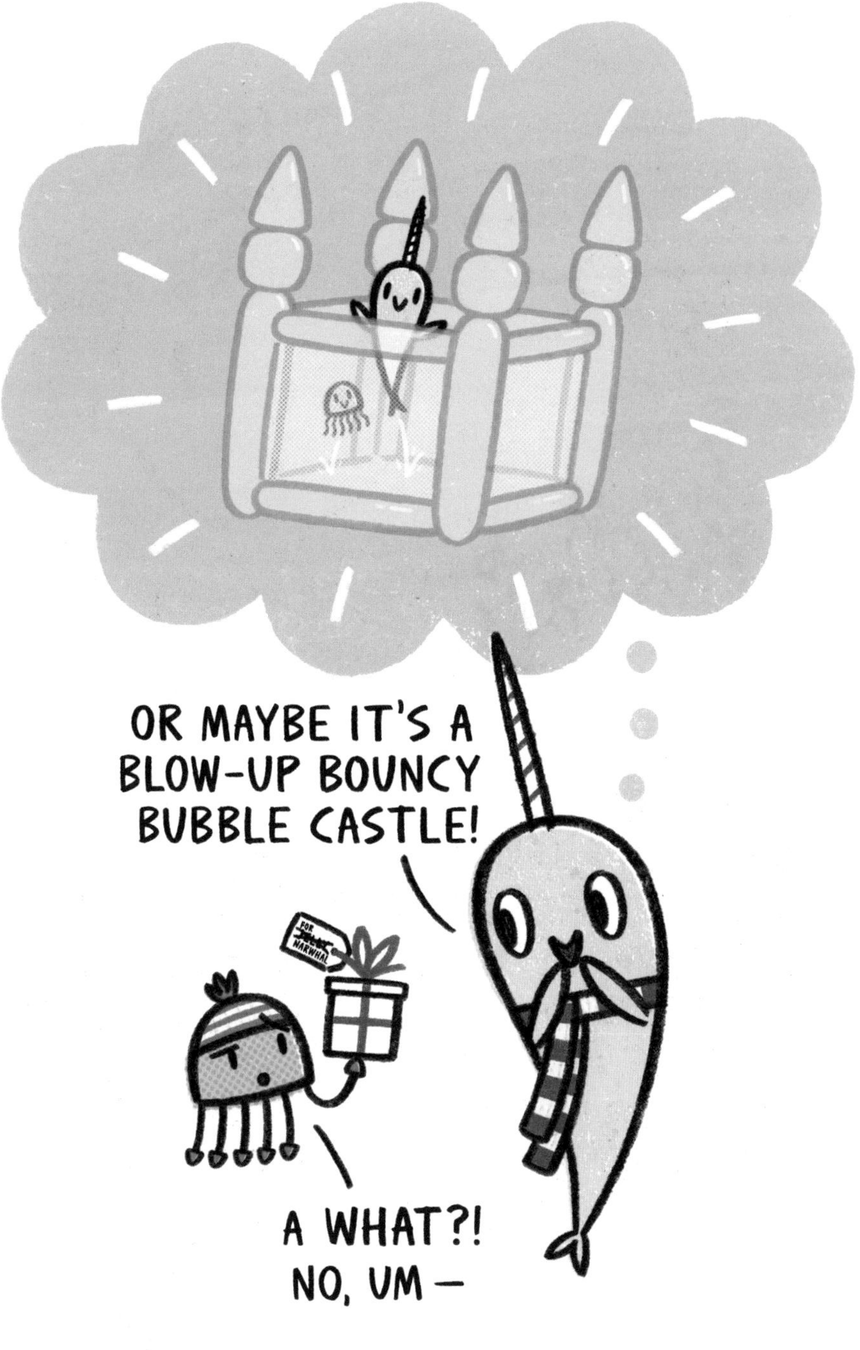

OR MAYBE IT'S A BLOW-UP BOUNCY BUBBLE CASTLE!
FOR
NARWHAL
A WHAT?! NO, UM –

NARWHAL, IT'S ACTUALLY —

WAIT! DON'T TELL ME. THIS IS THE **BEST** PRESENT _EVER!_

BECAUSE AS LONG AS I DON'T OPEN IT . . .

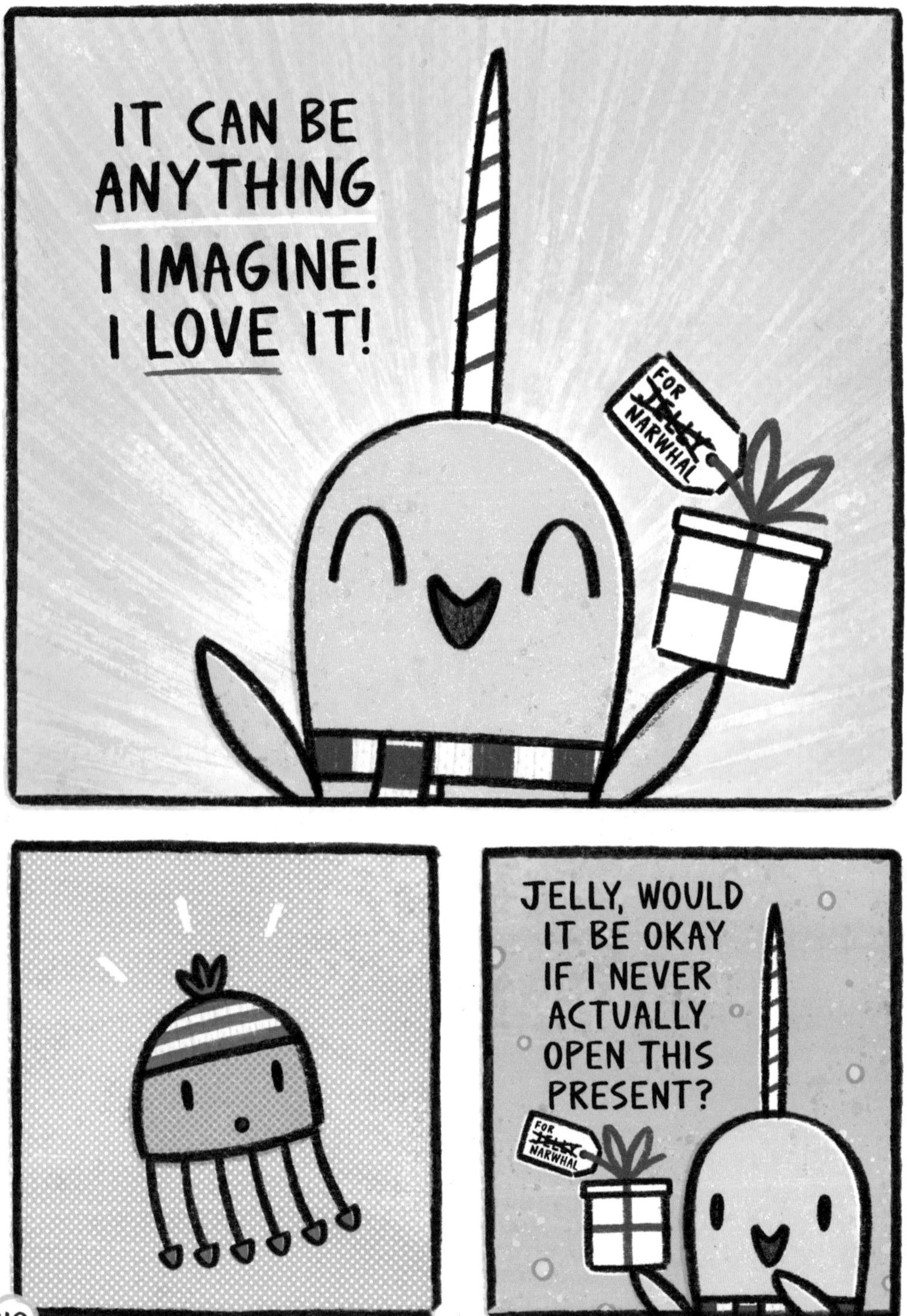
IT CAN BE ANYTHING I IMAGINE! I LOVE IT!
FOR
NARWHAL
JELLY, WOULD IT BE OKAY IF I NEVER ACTUALLY OPEN THIS PRESENT?
FOR
NARWHAL

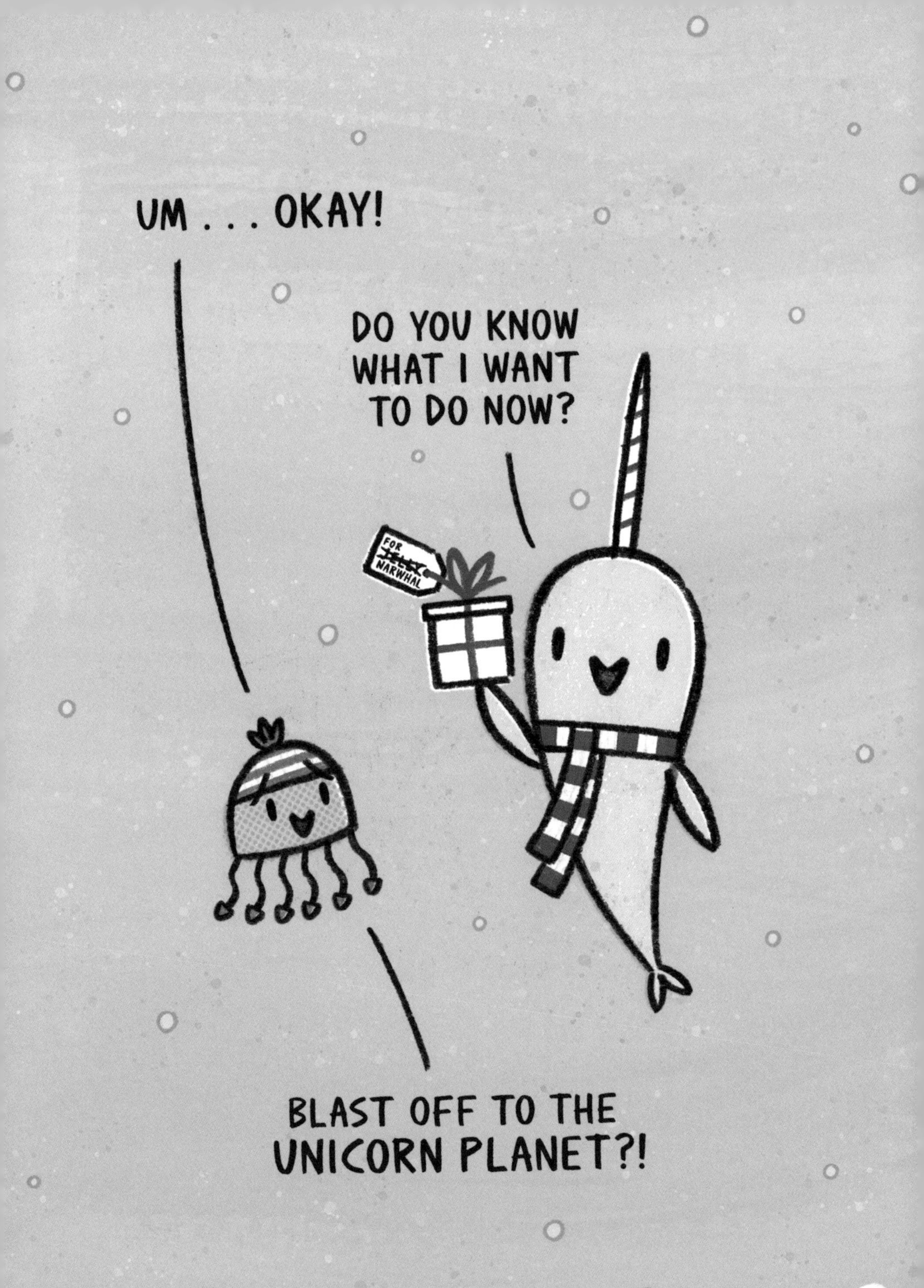
UM . . . OKAY!
DO YOU KNOW WHAT I WANT TO DO NOW?
FOR
NARWHAL
BLAST OFF TO THE UNICORN PLANET?!

NOPE! NOT YET, AT LEAST.
I THINK IT'S TIME TO COSY UP
WITH A GOOD BOOK AND A BEST BUD!
WANT TO MAKE A STORY?

SURE THING!

WRITE ON!

THE **MEAN** <u>GREEN</u>

JELLY BEAN

by Narwhal and Jelly

ONCE UPON A TIME, THERE WAS A TERRIBLY MEAN, AWFULLY GREEN JELLY BEAN. IT WAS VERY SOUR AND NOT AT ALL NICE.

HEY, HOW YOU BEAN? HAPPY HOLIDAYS!

BAH! BEAT IT!

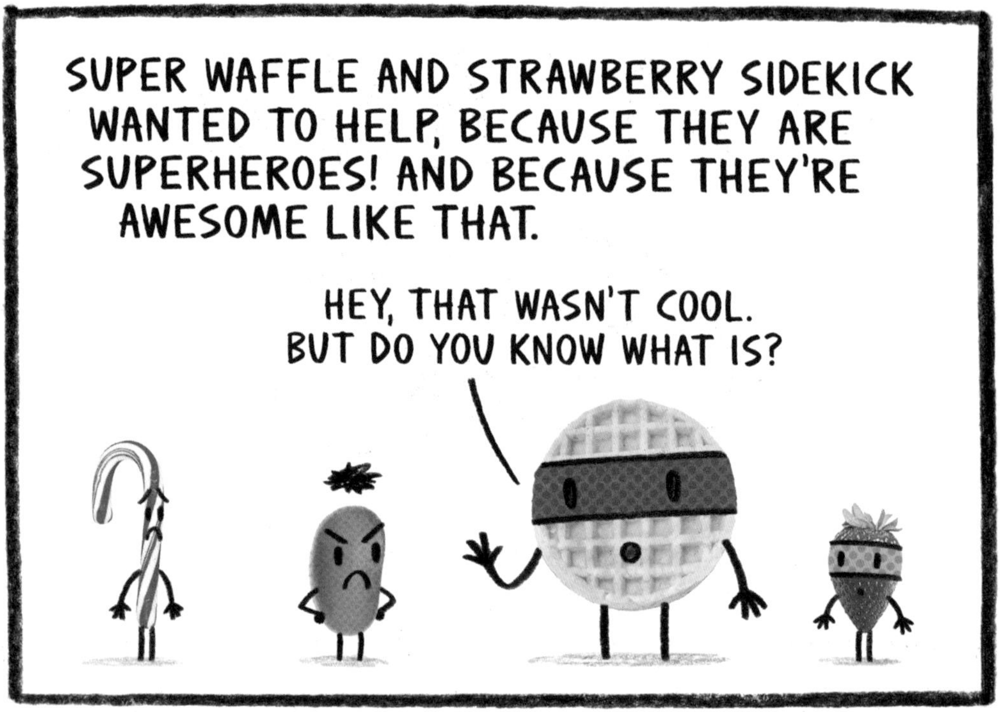
SUPER WAFFLE AND STRAWBERRY SIDEKICK WANTED TO HELP, BECAUSE THEY ARE SUPERHEROES! AND BECAUSE THEY'RE AWESOME LIKE THAT.
HEY, THAT WASN'T COOL. BUT DO YOU KNOW WHAT IS?

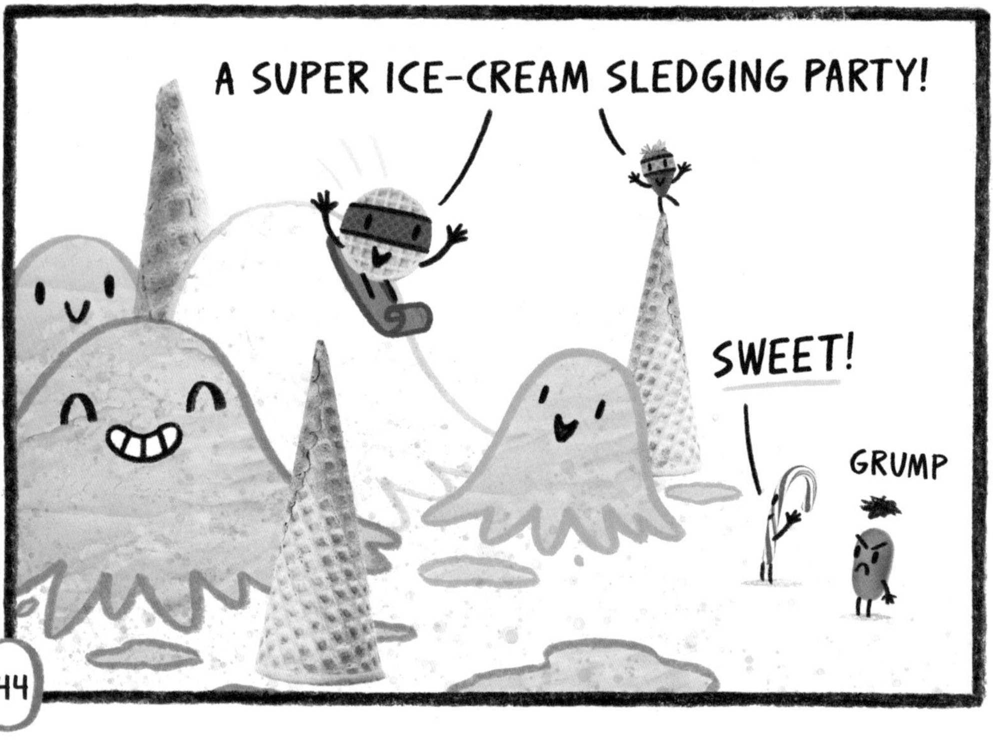
A SUPER ICE-CREAM SLEDGING PARTY!
SWEET!
GRUMP

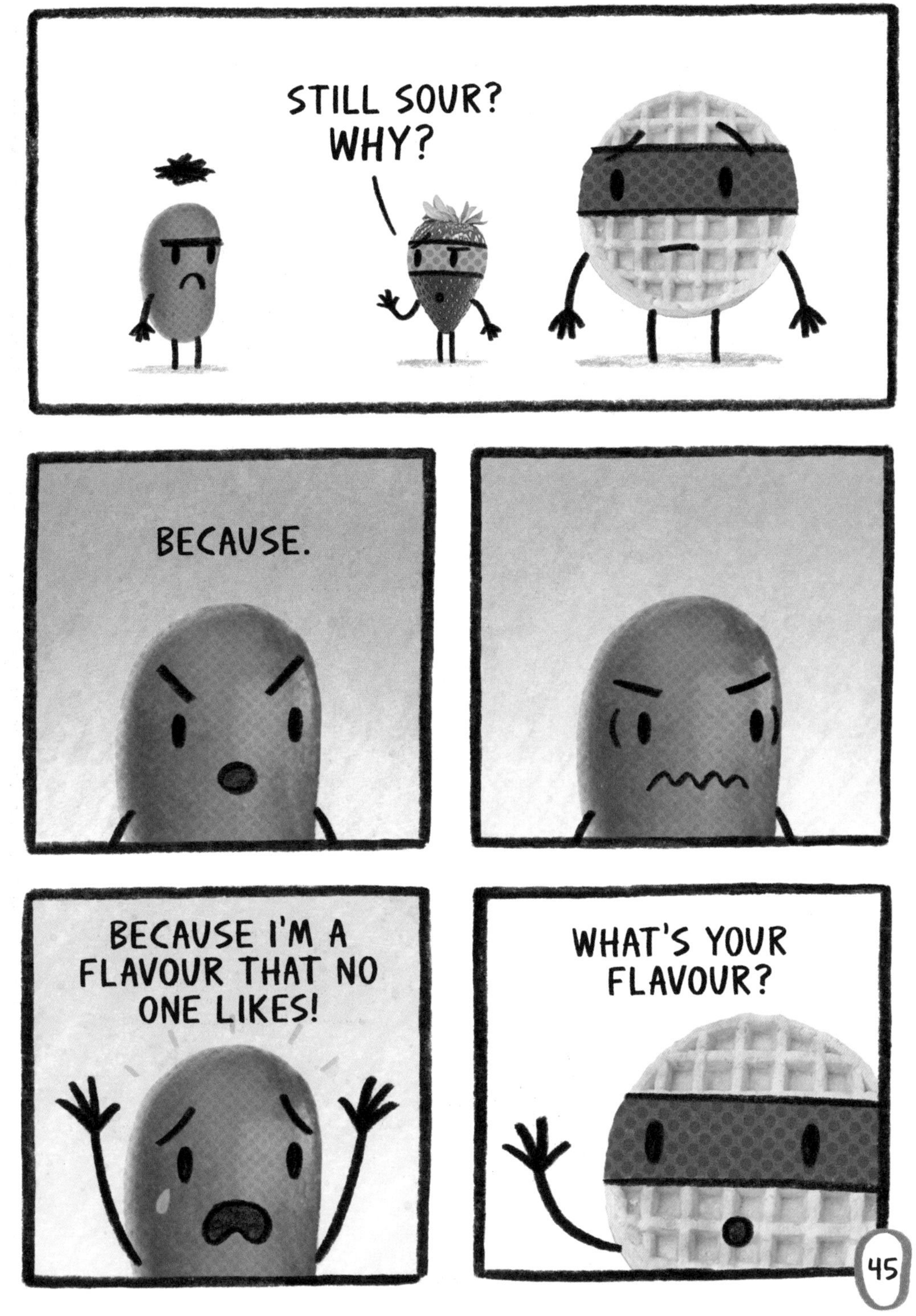
STILL SOUR?
WHY?
BECAUSE.
BECAUSE I'M A FLAVOUR THAT NO ONE LIKES!
WHAT'S YOUR FLAVOUR?

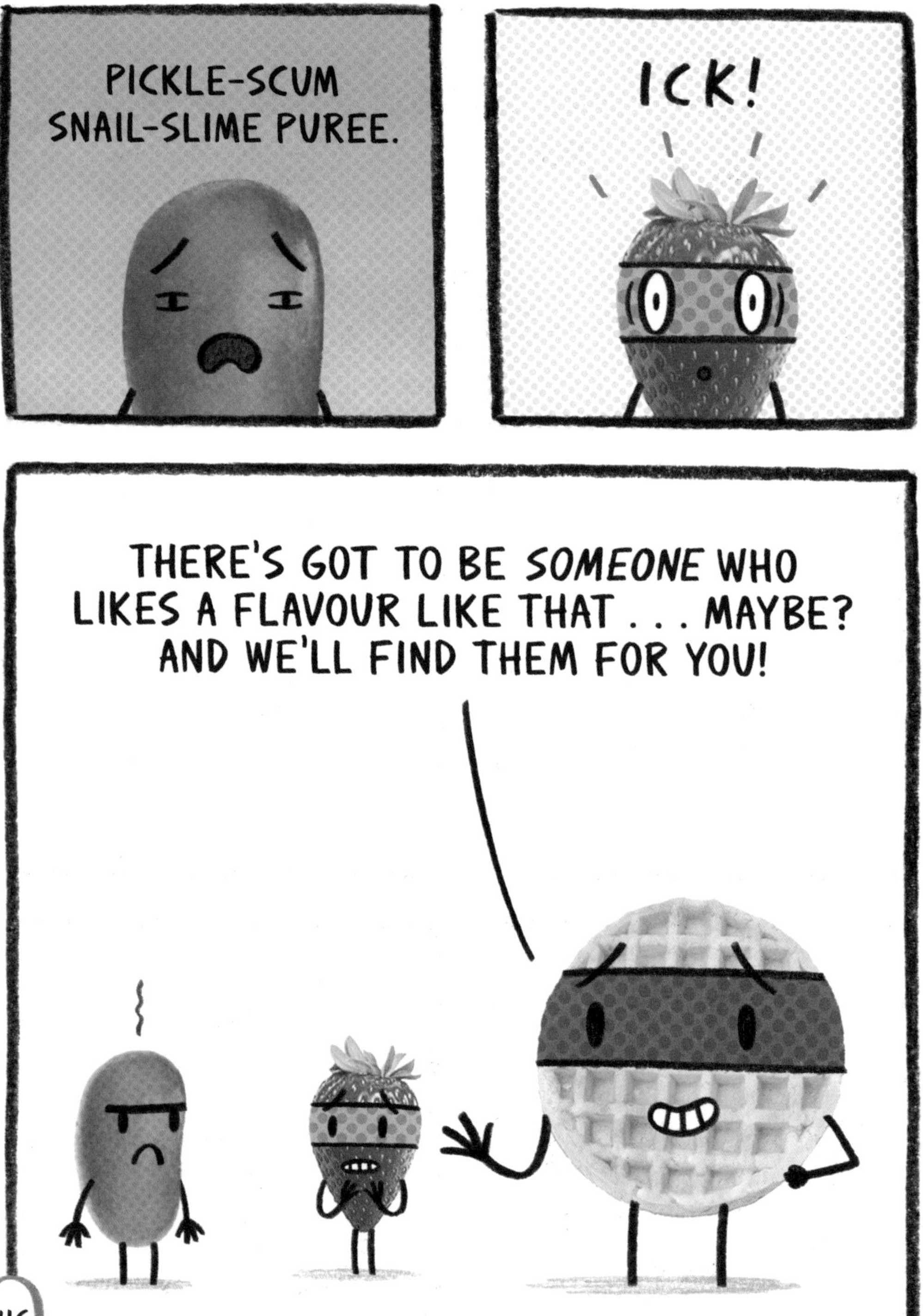
PICKLE-SCUM SNAIL-SLIME PUREE.
ICK!
THERE'S GOT TO BE *SOMEONE* WHO LIKES A FLAVOUR LIKE THAT . . . MAYBE? AND WE'LL FIND THEM FOR YOU!

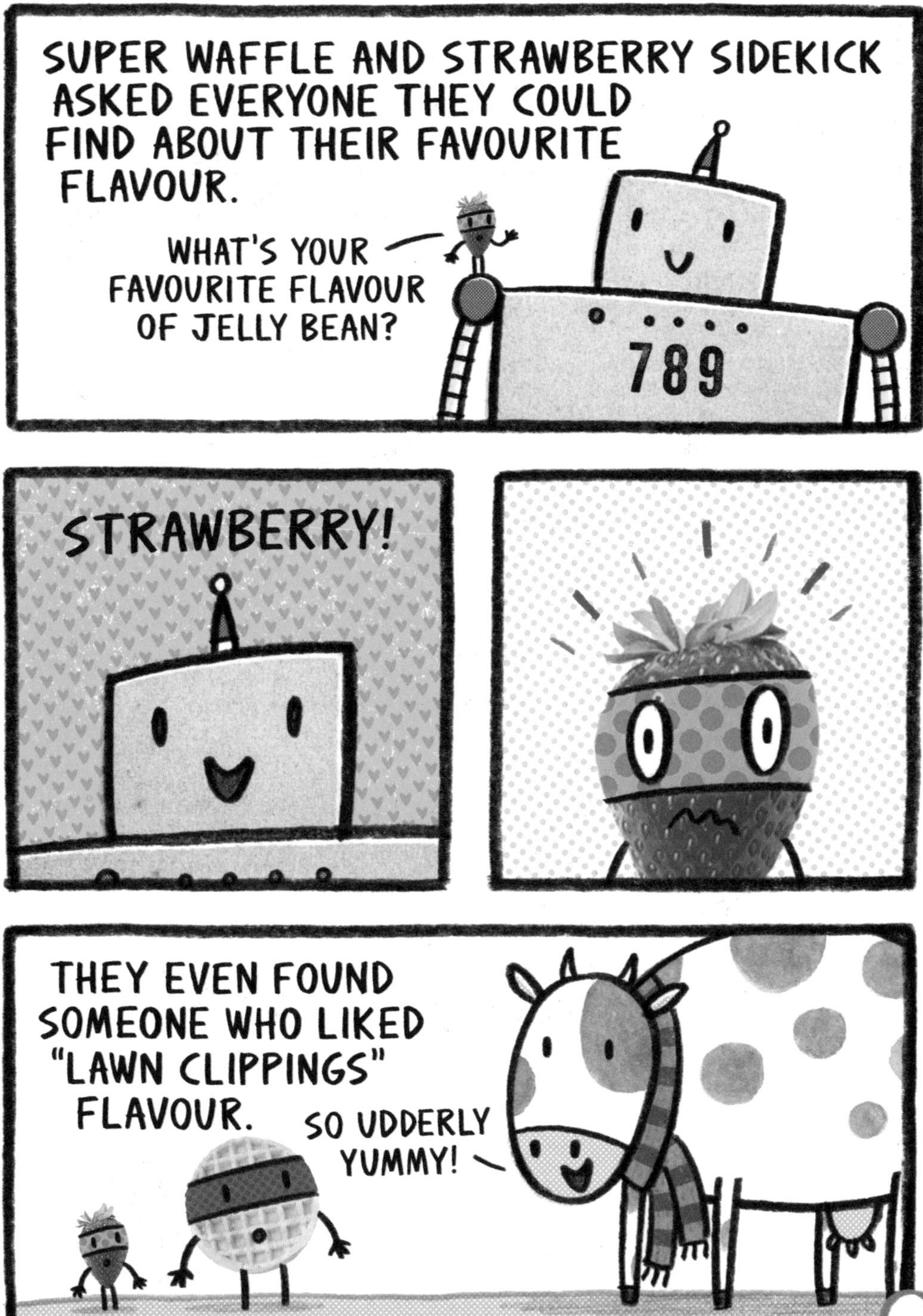
SUPER WAFFLE AND STRAWBERRY SIDEKICK ASKED EVERYONE THEY COULD FIND ABOUT THEIR FAVOURITE FLAVOUR.
WHAT'S YOUR FAVOURITE FLAVOUR OF JELLY BEAN?
789
STRAWBERRY!
THEY EVEN FOUND SOMEONE WHO LIKED "LAWN CLIPPINGS" FLAVOUR.
SO UDDERLY YUMMY!

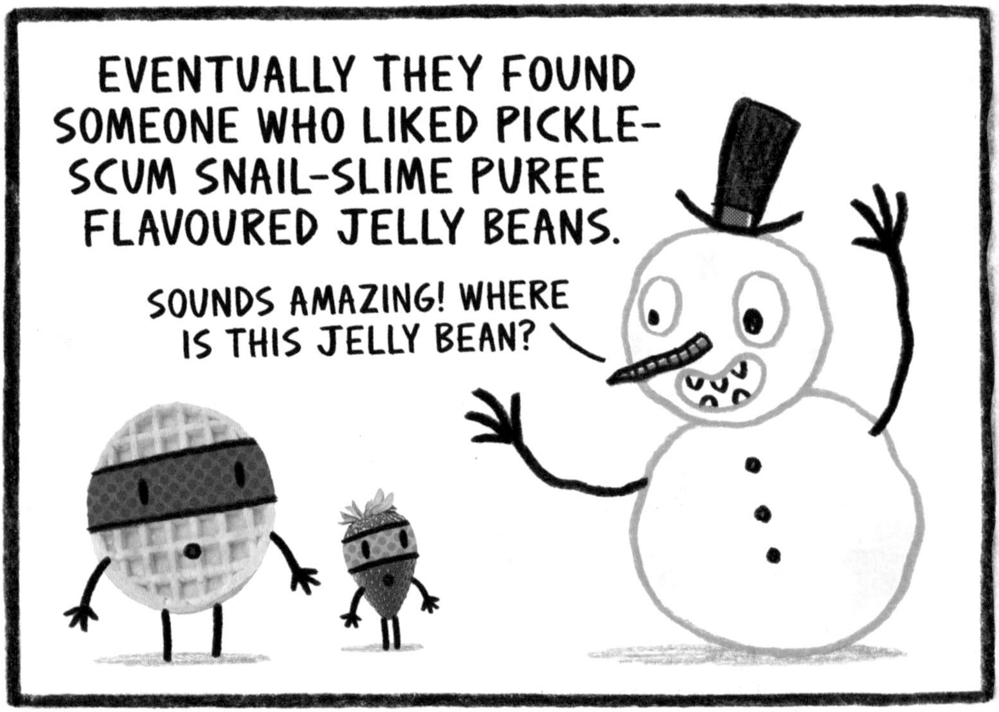
EVENTUALLY THEY FOUND SOMEONE WHO LIKED PICKLE-SCUM SNAIL-SLIME PUREE FLAVOURED JELLY BEANS.
SOUNDS AMAZING! WHERE IS THIS JELLY BEAN?

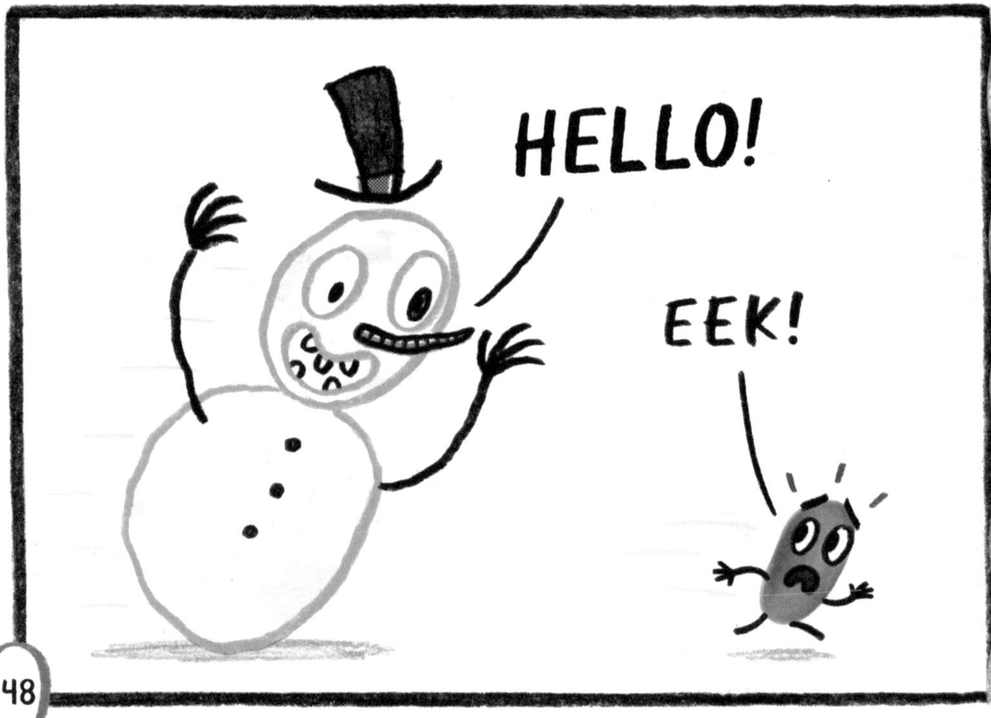
HELLO!
EEK!

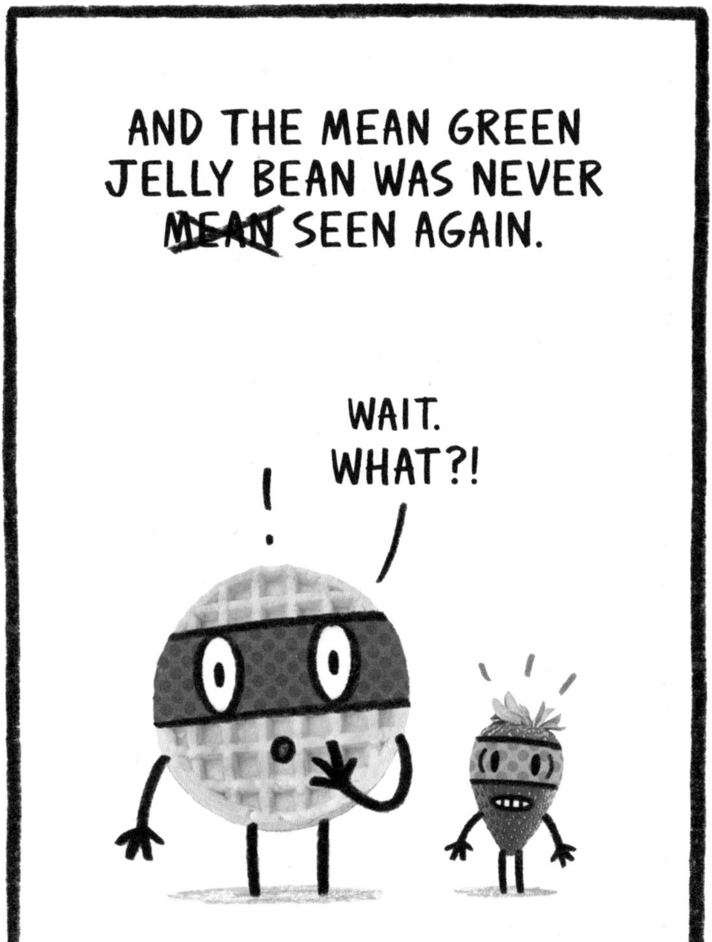
AND THE MEAN GREEN JELLY BEAN WAS NEVER ~~MEAN~~ SEEN AGAIN.
!
WAIT. WHAT?!

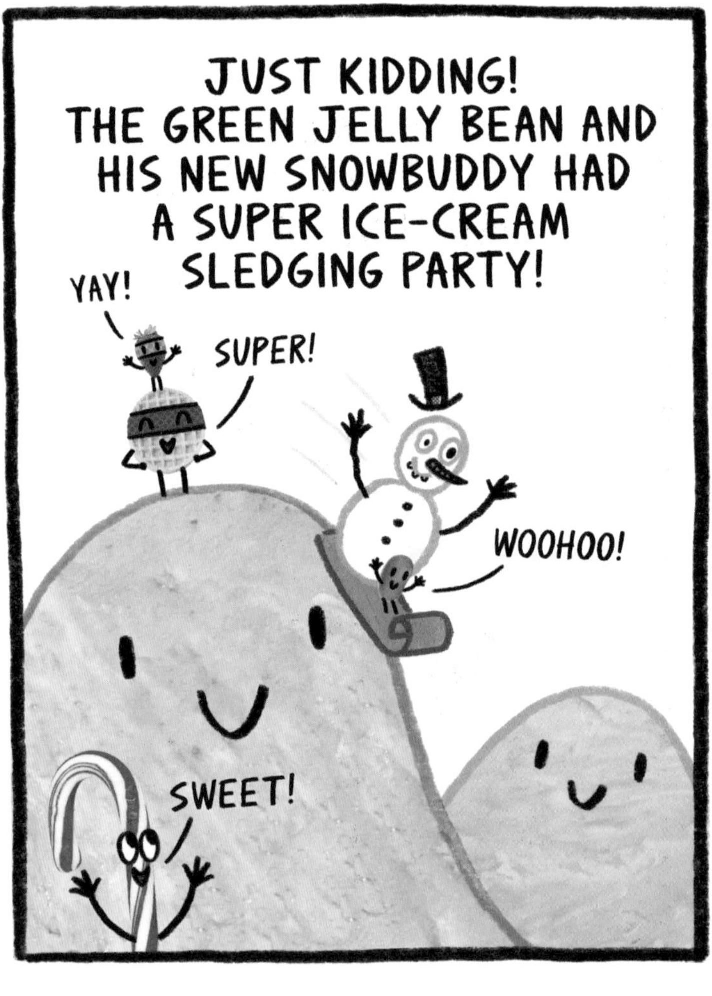
JUST KIDDING!
THE GREEN JELLY BEAN AND
HIS NEW SNOWBUDDY HAD
A SUPER ICE-CREAM
SLEDGING PARTY!
YAY!
SUPER!
WOOHOO!
SWEET!

THE
MERRY
MERMICORN!

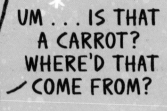

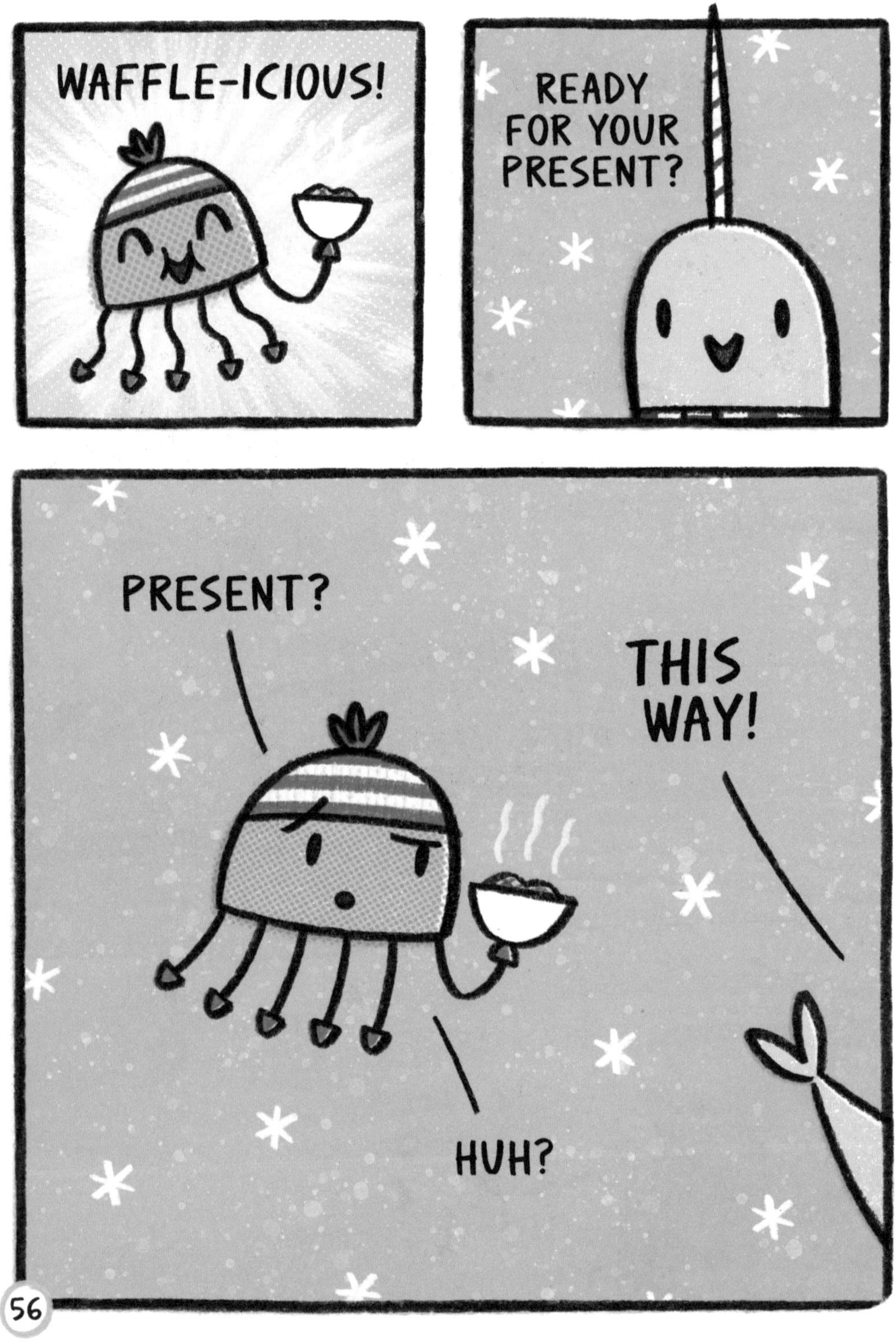
WAFFLE-ICIOUS!
READY FOR YOUR PRESENT?
PRESENT?
THIS WAY!
HUH?

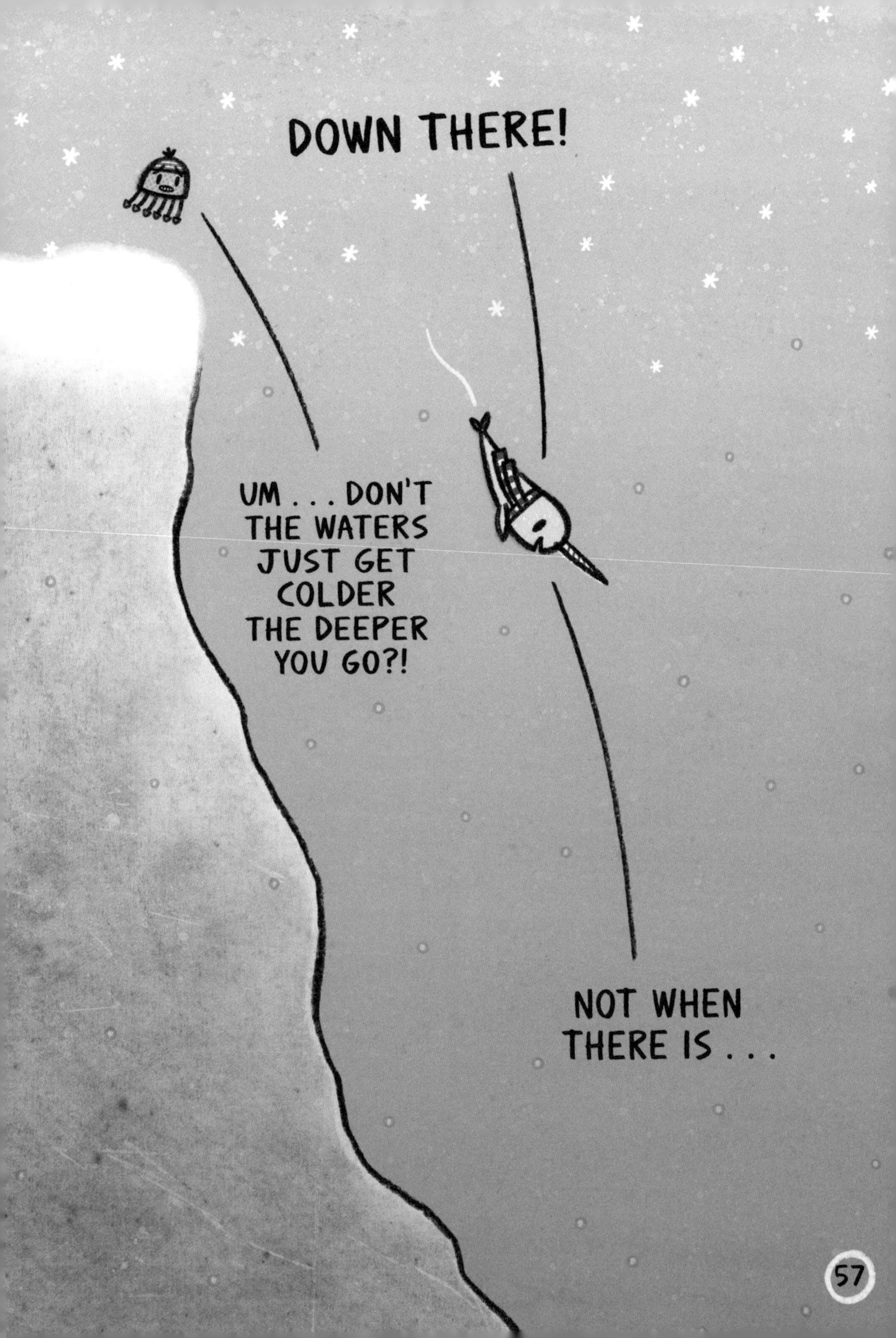
DOWN THERE!
UM . . . DON'T THE WATERS JUST GET COLDER THE DEEPER YOU GO?!
NOT WHEN THERE IS . . .

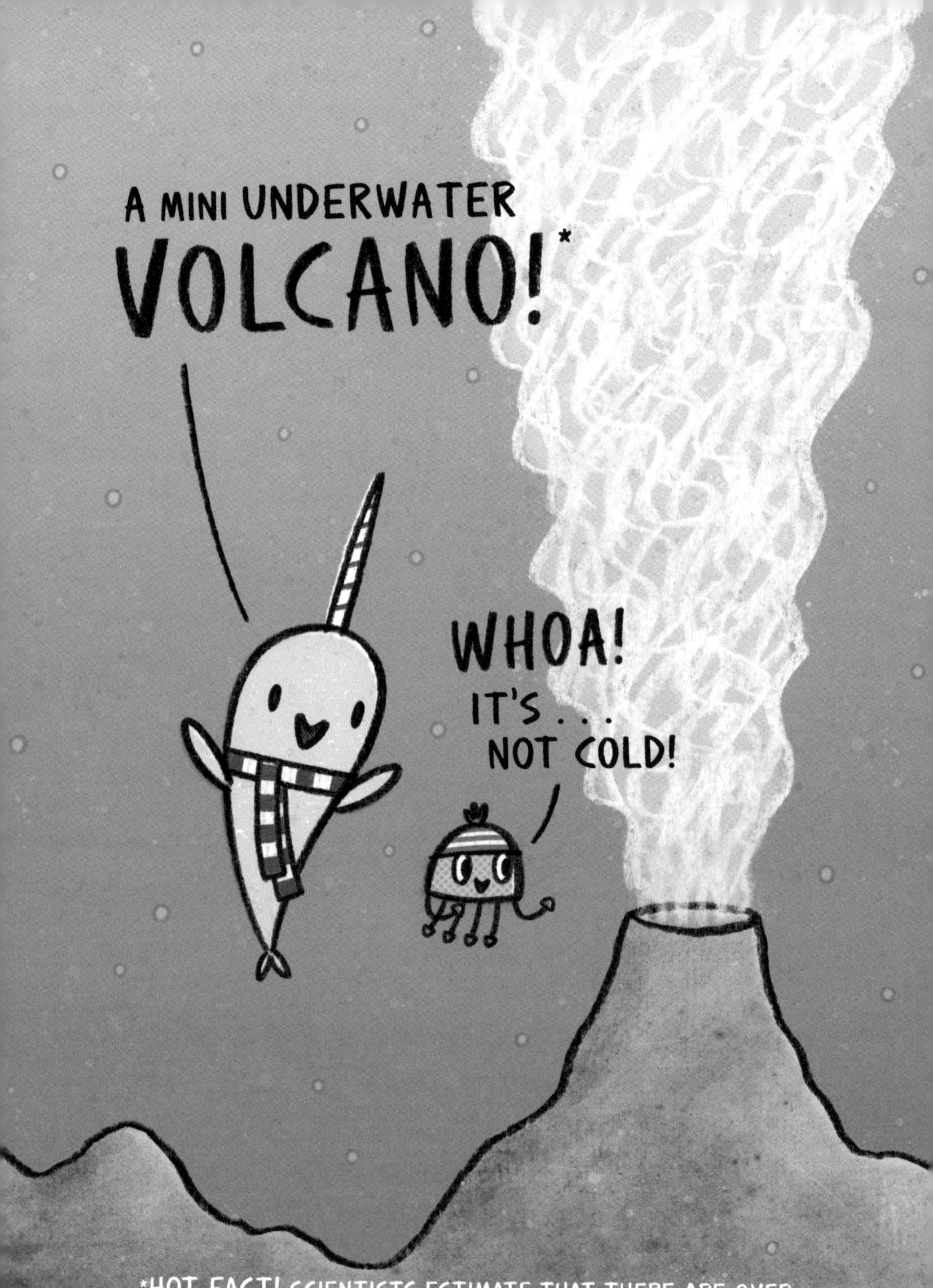
A MINI UNDERWATER VOLCANO!*
WHOA! IT'S . . . NOT COLD!

*HOT FACT! SCIENTISTS ESTIMATE THAT THERE ARE OVER A MILLION SUBMARINE VOLCANOES IN THE WORLD!

59

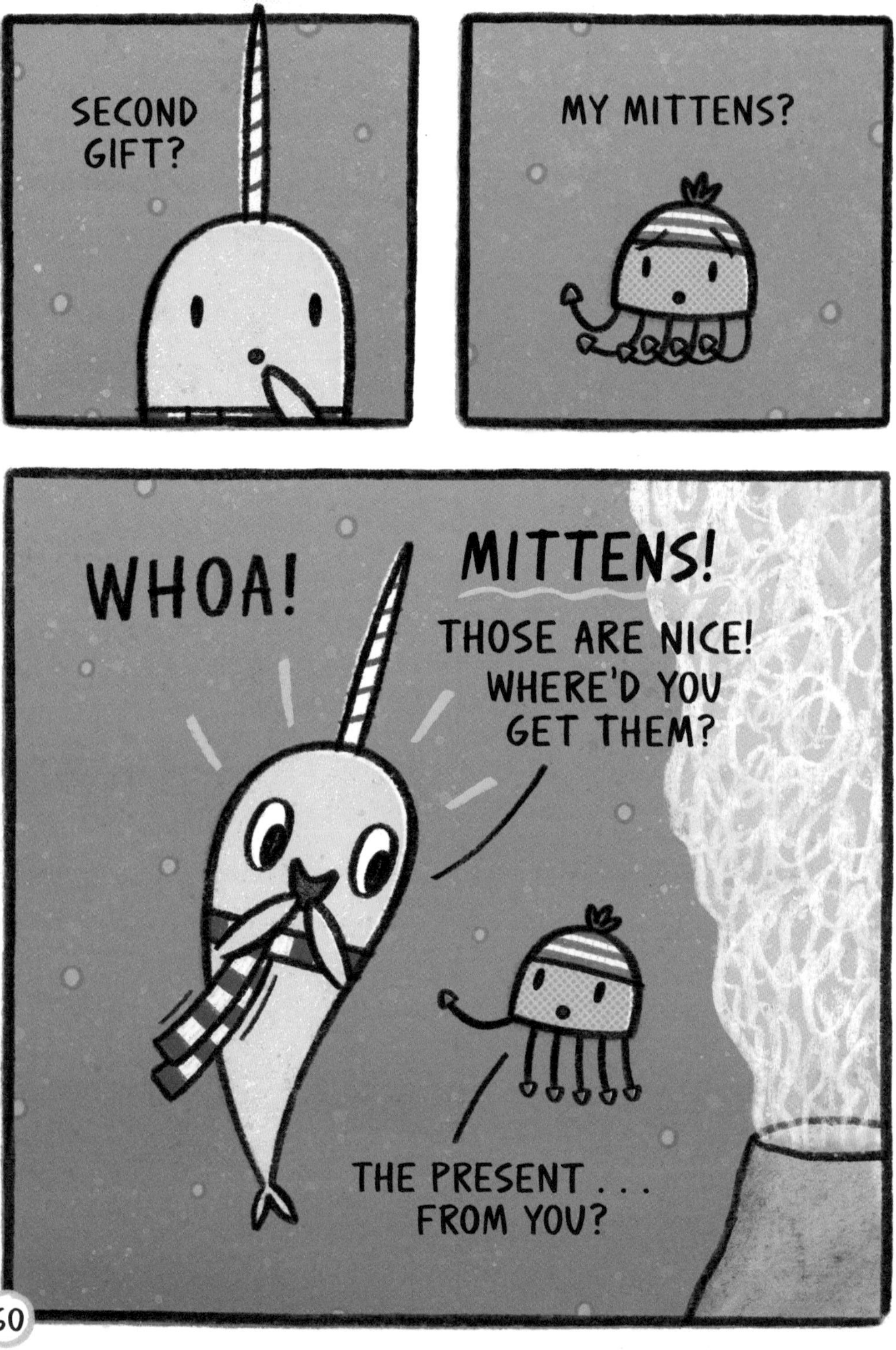
SECOND GIFT?
MY MITTENS?
WHOA!
MITTENS!
THOSE ARE NICE! WHERE'D YOU GET THEM?
THE PRESENT . . . FROM YOU?